KILL PATTON!

December 16, 1944: An American general is
marked for death! Nazi commandos
disguised as American GIs operate behind
lines, disrupting supply convoys and
communications, and preparing for a
special VIP murder! Were they planning to
the Supreme Allied Commander – or
could it be the famous 'cowboy' general
who led the tanks?

KILL PATTON!

KILL PATTON!

by

Charles Whiting

Dales Large Print Books
Long Preston, North Yorkshire,
BD23 4ND, England.

British Library Cataloguing in Publication Data.

Whiting, Charles
    Kill Patton!

    A catalogue record of this book is
    available from the British Library

    ISBN   978-1-84262-609-2 pbk

First published in 1974

Copyright © Charles Whiting 1974

Cover illustration © Mary Evans' Picture Library

The moral right of the author has been asserted

Published in Large Print 2008 by arrangement with
Eskdale Publishing

Dales Large Print is an imprint of Library Magna Books Ltd.

Printed and bound in Great Britain by
T.J. (International) Ltd., Cornwall, PL28 8RW

BOOK ONE: GRAB!

DAY ONE:
SATURDAY, 16 DECEMBER, 1944

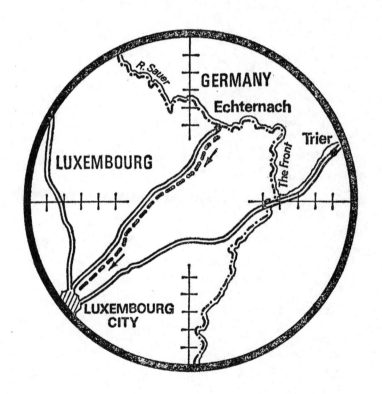

I

It was bitterly cold. The GI guarding the roadblock stamped his feet on the snow and buried his face deep in his greatcoat collar. Another forty minutes and his relief would be coming up the road from the little Luxembourg border-town of Echternach.

Behind him in the first row of blacked-out houses the door of the Café Texas flew open for a moment. There was a brief snatch of tinny accordion music and the excited laughter of the whores who catered for enlisted men. Then all was silence again.

The GI stared up at the black outline of the Ferschweiler Plateau beyond the little river which marked the border with Germany. Somewhere up there in the crumbling cliff-top abbey was the enemy. But nothing had been seen of the Germans since the Fourth Division had struggled back from the hell of the Huertgen Forest in November with over seven thousand casualties. Occasionally at night the sentries of the single infantry company stationed in Echternach heard the rattle of a tank or the clip-clop of a horse which the Germans used to draw their artillery, but that was all. This was the ghost front where nothing ever happened, and to which General Hodges, commanding the US 1st Army, ordered his shattered divisions for refitting and his green ones for realistic combat training.

Suddenly in the distance the young GI heard what sounded like the steady plop-plop of a two-stroke motorbike. Staring upwards, he saw a faint unhurried speck of red against the night sky. Instinctively he pulled his helmet down more firmly and pressed himself closer to the barricade. It was a buzz bomb.

Carrying nearly a ton of high explosive, it chugged on towards Antwerp. In the direction of the capital, searchlights flicked on, poking stiff white fingers into the sky. Now, the bomb was directly overhead and the sentry could see its red trail quite distinctly.

The buzz bomb disappeared, the searchlights went out and the sentry looked at his watch again. Another ten minutes. But twenty-year-old Private First Class Ed Kirk was fated never to be relieved. At that moment a shadowy figure emerged from the ruins of the bridge over the River Sauer. Startled by the noise, Kirk made to free his rifle from his shoulder but his movements were hampered by his gloves and in an instant an arm held his throat in a vice-like grip and a knife slid noiselessly into his ribs. Cautiously the shadow relaxed his grip and Kirk's knees buckled under him. Carefully, he looked up the road. The tinny music was still coming from the *Ami* café. Clearly they were too busy with their whores to be bothered about fighting the war. He bent down and wiped the blood off his knife on the dead man's greatcoat, then straightened up and gave a low whistle. '*Alles klan,*' he whispered.

Half a dozen figures, their faces blackened like his, thick socks drawn over their jackboots, stole from the shadows. Swiftly they spread out to cover the shell-holed road which led to the ruined bridge, their Schmeisser machine pistols at the ready.

An SS officer followed them, glancing at the body of the GI sprawled in the snow. 'Good work, Krause,' he whispered, then threw a quick look at the protective screen. 'Keep your eyes open,' he ordered.

'*Jahwohl, Oberstuermbannfuehrer,*' the killer answered.

Satisfied with his security, the young lieutenant hurried back to the river, paused and whistled softly three times. At the agreed signal, dark figures emerged from the tree-lined track at the edge of the cliff on the other side. 'All right,' he called. 'You can begin bringing it across now.'

Krause joined him at the bank and together they watched as the engineers freed the straw from the tank's tracks. They had used straw to deaden the noise when bringing it up the

13

night before. Two of them then waded through the knee-high water, dragging the towing ropes behind them. The planners had picked the spot well, and they made it easily. Moments later the rest followed them and seized the ropes.

'Now,' the sergeant in charge ordered. There was a rusty rattle, and the thirty-ton tank began to move towards the river.

Krause looked at the young officer. 'What do you make of it, *Oberstuerm?*' he asked with the easy camaraderie of the *Waffen SS*.

The lieutenant shrugged. 'It doesn't do to ask too many questions, Krause.' He hesitated, uncertain what he should tell the NCO. 'In Trier, they said it had something to do with the new offensive. Anyway, we'll show those *Ami* bastards that we still have plenty of fight in us.'

Krause agreed dutifully, but he was no longer sure. He remembered how his division, *Das Reich,* had left the horror of the Normandy battlefields, sneaking out at night like thieves, with two-thirds of their tanks gone and a lot of good men dead.

The engineers had got the tank across the river now and the men on the ropes gave one last great heave as the tank rumbled up the bank and came to a stop on the road. The engineer who had been operating the tiller rods climbed out of the driver's seat and slapped its metal surface contemptuously. 'Breathe hard on the bitch and she'll go up in flames,' he said. The tank was an American Sherman.

The lieutenant said nothing. He well knew what a fire trap the Sherman was. He had been with Panzer Meyer in Normandy when the SS general had put twenty of them out of action single-handed. Walking over to the captured tank with Krause he said, 'You check the other side, I'll do this.'

'Yes, *Oberstuerm*,' Krause said dutifully.

The newly painted yellow, red and blue triangle with the '4' of the Fourth Armoured Division in its centre looked okay. Krause ran his fingers over the plugged and painted spot where an armour-piercing shell had penetrated the metal just outside Aachen three months before. No one would spot it. He paused and looked over the clutter of ammo boxes, bedrolls, helmets and camouflage nets attached to the deck. Everything seemed in order.

But the lieutenant was a thorough man. 'Krause, get those engineers over here. That's got to come off.' He pointed to the strip of tank track attached to the tank's glacis plate just below the 75-mm gun.

'Why, sir?'

'Because that cowboy general who runs the American Third Army doesn't allow his men to litter their tanks with extra armour for protection. Says the additional weight lowers their speed.'

'Well, if I were driving one of those bastards, *Obersturm*, I'd have every bit of protection I could find, including my metal shaving mirror.'

But Krause did as he was told. Six of the engineers swiftly lowered the length of track and tossed it into the ditch. The young officer urged them on. The dead man's relief would be coming out in exactly three minutes. The officer had been timing the relief for the last seven nights, and the *Amis* were punctual. 'All right,' he said, as soon as they were finished. 'Get back across the river.'

They splashed back and disappeared into the woods where the infantry in white camouflage suits were waiting nervously for zero hour. When the last engineer was out of sight the lieutenant flashed twice on his little blue torch.

Krause knew why. When Giskes of the *Abwehr* had briefed them at Trier, he had emphasised that they should make sure the infantry and engineers knew as little as possible about the operation. A few moments later they came wading through the water, stamping up the bank in their soft rubber-soled *Ami* boots. There were four of them, all dressed in American combat jackets with the same leather helmets the *Ami* tankers wore on their heads. Their leader, a sergeant, nodded to the lieutenant, 'Thank

16

you, you did a good job.'

'You've got two minutes left,' the lieutenant said.

'Good.' The sergeant turned to the other three. 'You can mount up.'

'Roger,' the smallest of the three answered in perfect English, and clambered into the driving seat. He was followed by a squarely built, ugly Tech/Five, who rolled when he walked like a sailor. 'Get a load of the name,' he said, as he reached up for a hand-hold, indicating the name painted on the turret. *'Gruesome Twosome.'* His ugly face broke into a good-humoured grin.

The man behind him grinned too. 'They must have known about your ugly mug,' he said. 'Get on with it,' the sergeant snapped. He followed them up on the turret. 'All right *Oberstuerm,* we're ready.'

There was one minute left now before the relief appeared. The young officer pulled out his duty whistle and blew a shrill blast.

There was an answering blast from somewhere on the top of the plateau. The sergeant snapped out an order in English. It was followed by the cough of the Sherman's engine. Clouds of smoke fogged the icy air. The sergeant on the turret said something into the throat mike and the tank started to move forward.

Over on the plateau, 'Moaning Minnie', the six-barrelled electrically operated mortar, roared into action. The shells tore through the night air, drowning the noise of the tank, and exploded in red and yellow balls of fire somewhere beyond the town. Another salvo followed and the lieutenant knew that it would continue firing for another four minutes – until the tank was clear of the road.

The tank rumbled on, passing over the body of the dead GI. Krause stared after it, shocked by the sergeant's deliberate brutality. He could easily have ordered the driver to go round the body. But there was no time to worry about the sergeant's callousness now. The mortar 'stonk' would end in a minute and by then they would have to be back on the other side of the river. 'All right,' he shouted above the howl of the mortar, 'fall back now!'

They needed no urging. They had all been with him in the hell of the Normandy fighting. They'd had a noseful of the war and they wanted no part of what was to come. Thankfully they waded back across the Sauer to their own lines where the tense young infantrymen, the last scrapings of the barrel, were waiting for the order to advance.

'Jesus H Christ!' the relief breathed in horror as he stared down at the thing which had once been his buddy Kirk.

The body was pressed flat, like a figure in a comic strip, the arms of its khaki uniform

18

at right angles to the flattened greatcoat. The brown combat boots and khaki pants were just as flat and thin, as if they had been cut from a sheet of dirty cardboard.

'What the hell happened?'

The top sergeant did not answer. He stared at the firs lining the other side of the river, as if looking for the answer to the question there.

'Do you think the mortar got him?' the relief asked. 'Don't talk crap,' the sergeant snorted. 'Get up to that goddam whorehouse, and tell them guys to get their britches on and haul their asses down here – pronto! Then get over to the captain's billet, get him out of the sack and tell him what happened to Kirk.'

'But why, Sarge?'

'Because son,' the sergeant answered, drawing his '45 and facing the dark outline of the Ferschweiler Plateau, 'we're in for trouble soon – plenty of trouble.'

II

The four-star general, whose wide grin was known to the whole western world through the papers and newsreels, leaned forward to the smiling sergeant, holding the bride's hand as if someone were going to pull her away from him and said above the noise, 'Okay Mickey, do you mind if I kiss the bride?'

'No, you don't, General.' It was 'Tex' Lee, the booming-voiced bespectacled captain who kept the general's records straight. 'I gave her away and I get first kiss, even if she is a sergeant.' There was a ripple of laughter among the guests at the wedding reception.

Tex leaned forward and planted a hearty kiss on the bride's face, as she stood there at Mickey's side looking very unmilitary in her white wedding gown. 'Now it's your turn, General,' he said.

The general gave her a resounding kiss. 'That's the first time I've ever kissed a sergeant,' he said.

There was a cheer from the uniformed audience. One of the two bridesmaids, Sue Sarafin, dressed in her usual WAC uniform, began to sniff, but her snivels were drowned by the pop of the first champagne cork. Soon they were popping everywhere, and the guests started to make their way to the buffet table.

The general beamed. Everything was going fine. Two hours earlier he had been informed that President Roosevelt had nominated him a five-star general, the first man ever to hold the rank. Even Pershing, the World War One commander of the AEF, had remained a four-star general. Monty had written to him asking for Christmas leave, which he had granted – so that particular thorn was out of his flesh for a couple of days. Everything was quiet at the front, and now Pearlie and Mickey were enjoying themselves in spite of the freezing cold in the Versailles Palace, where the wedding ceremony was being held.

'Here, sir, another glass of champagne.' It was Kay Summersby, the British girl who had become an intimate member of the 'family' with which he had surrounded himself during the past two years.

'Thanks, Kay,' he said. 'I'd prefer a bourbon and water, though.'

'I could get you one.'

He shook his head. 'It's okay. I've got a conference with Brad in an hour. I'll finish this and be off. If you would, you might tell Tex to get the car.'

She nodded. 'All right, sir.' She turned and walked over to where Tex was talking with one of the few British officers who had turned up for the wedding. Although they had all been invited the British did not seem to like the easy informality of Supreme Headquarters.

He put his glass down and the professionals, who had been watching him all the time out of the corner of their eyes, put their glasses down also and stood up. He motioned to them to sit down. Not for nothing was 'Ike' known as the US Army's Number One Democratic Soldier. One day the wedding reception and everything that went with it would gain him a few more votes. But that day was still a long way off.

'Well, what do you think, Brad?' Bedell Smith asked. 'Do you think Hodges is going to pull off the attack on the Roer.'

Bradley, the commander of the US 12th Army, nodded and answered Eisenhower's Chief-of-Staff in his careful, somewhat plodding way. 'Well, the terrain is terrible, as you know, and the Krauts' flooding the area isn't helping any, also we're getting terribly short of replacements.' He tugged at his steel-rimmed glasses. 'That's what this conference is about, isn't it, Ike?' He glanced over at Eisenhower who sat at the head of the table in the Versailles map room, at which were grouped the six participants of the vital replacement conference.

Eisenhower nodded, but did not interfere. Let 'Beetle' take care of it, he told himself. The red-haired, terrible-tempered Chief-of-Staff, permanently plagued by his stomach ulcers, could play the devil's advocate much better than he ever could. He settled back and listened attentively while the Chief-of-Staff pressed Brad for further details of what his Army Group was doing to find more riflemen for the depleted ranks of the frontline outfits.

The afternoon conference droned on. Slightly before four they were interrupted by a tap on the door. It was Brigadier Betts, the Deputy Chief-of-Intelligence. Eisenhower frowned across at his Chief-of-Intelligence, Brigadier Kenneth Strong. Strong, a regular officer in the British army, rose hurriedly. Like everyone else at Supreme Headquarters he knew that when Ike 'blew his top', as the Americans phrased it, he could be very unpredictable.

'What is it Tom?' he whispered.

'Trouble in the Ardennes, Ken.'

'The Ardennes! Nothing's happened there since September.'

'There has now.' He struck the pile of top secret intelligence reports in his hand. 'They've been coming in all afternoon, ever since the conference started. As usual they're contradictory – they always are when trouble starts. But a dozen outfits have reported contact with the enemy in the area in the last hour, and they can't all be imagining Krauts, can they?'

'Do you think the balloon's going up?'

'I don't know, Ken, but my guess is that it is. We've been asking for trouble in the Ardennes for months now, you know that. Four divisions to hold a line of seventy-odd miles and three of those green or virtually green.' He pulled a hastily prepared map from the sheaf of intelligence reports. 'The best we could do in the time available, but it'll give you an idea of the position.' Hurriedly he began to brief his superior officer on the situation, while behind them the five men at the conference table waited with mounting curiosity.

Finally Eisenhower spoke. He was more curious than angry at this strange interruption. 'What is it, Ken?'

Strong walked back into the room, while Betts closed the door. 'Gentlemen,' he said formally, 'the enemy has counter-attacked at five separate points across the First Army sector!'

'Beetle' was the first to break the ensuing silence. 'We told you, Brad, that the Krauts might have a crack at you through the Ardennes.' He nodded at Strong. 'Ken here even came to your headquarters to warn you.'

Bradley's eyes gleamed behind his steel-rimmed glasses, but when he spoke his voice was calm. 'Hell, the other fellow knows that he must lighten the pressure Patton has built up against him. If by coming through the Ardennes he can force us to pull Patton's troops out of the Saar and throw them against his counter-offensive, he'll get what he's after. And that,' he concluded, pleased with *his* reaction to the news, 'is just a little more time.'

Eisenhower hesitated a moment. The grin was gone now. His high forehead was creased in a worried frown. 'This is no local attack, Brad,' he said slowly. 'It isn't logical for the Germans to launch a local attack at our weakest point.'

'If it's not a local attack,' Bradley replied a little hotly, 'what kind of attack is it?'

Eisenhower shrugged. 'That remains to be seen. But I don't think we can afford to sit on our hands till we've found out.'

'What do you think we should do, then?' Bradley asked, slightly mollified that Ike had not continued 'Beetle's' attack on his Ardennes strategy.

'Send Middleton some help. I'd say two armoured divisions.'

'I suppose,' Bradley said slowly, 'that it *would* be safer that way. Of course, you know that one of those divisions will have to come from Patton.'

Ike flushed slightly. 'So?' His voice was suddenly icy.

Bradley did not notice the signs; he was too concerned with the problem of trying to get two divisions from his brilliant subordinate, who had been his commanding officer until a year ago in Sicily when he had slapped a GI for supposed malingering and had lost the top job of commander of all US invasion forces in Europe. 'Georgie won't like losing a division a few days before his big attack on the Saar.'

Eisenhower exploded. 'You tell him,' he snorted, 'that Ike is running this damned war!'

Bradley pushed back his chair and hurried to the phone. One minute later he was speaking to Patton at his command post in Nancy. 'George,' he said after a few explanatory remarks, 'get the 10th Armored on the road to Luxembourg City.'

The line crackled with the 3rd Army Commander's objections.

Bradley explained the situation once again patiently. Patton was his star army commander. He could not afford to offend him.

'But goddammit,' Patton cursed, 'there's no major threat up there! That's just a goddam little spoiling attack. They want to throw us off balance down here. Make me stop my offensive!'

Bradley knew he might be right; it was too soon yet to tell. But he couldn't afford to take any chances, especially with Ike on his back. 'I hate like hell to do it, George,' he said, 'but I've got to have that division. Even if it's only a spoiling attack as you say, Middleton must have help.'

Patton uttered an obscenity, but Bradley cut him off with a curt order and returned to the map room where the other four were now crowded round the big wall map, at which the Chief-of-Intelligence was sketching in the information given to him by Betts.

Bradley listened attentively until the brigadier finished his exposé. For a moment there was silence while they all absorbed the information, pondering over the personal implications of the new situation. Strong watched them carefully. Then he cleared his throat. 'There is one other thing, gentlemen,' he announced. He touched the pile of flimsies which Betts had given him. 'Apart from everything else, Colonel Sheen of my counter-intelligence staff has just had two separate incidents reported to him, which might mean something.' He shrugged. 'Or nothing.'

He pulled out a flimsy from the bottom of the pile. 'A military police unit stationed in Liège – Liège, *Belgium,*' he added for the benefit of his American listeners, who, he found, always named the country after the town, 'reports – and I quote, "German SS officer picked up near the River Meuse wearing US uniform and carrying forged US identification. Mission unknown. Presently being grilled."' He put the flimsy away carefully and selected another one.

'This one comes from a British Thirty Corps tank unit stationed on the other side of the Meuse at Dinant, where the bridge is, if you remember, gentlemen?'

The bridges at Huy and Dinant below

Liège were the only ones across the Meuse capable of carrying heavy traffic. They would be the obvious targets for the Germans if they ever got that far into the Ardennes.

Strong skipped the officialese of the heading and read the message: '"In an attempt to run a roadblock just outside town, a jeep containing four American soldiers was blown up by a gammon mine. At first it was thought that this was another wartime accident. On further investigation, however, it was discovered that the four dead men were wearing the uniform of the *Waffen SS* under their American clothing. All were armed and possessed large sums of Allied currency to a total of ten thousand US dollars." Obviously the Germans are trying to penetrate our lines. The question remains – why?' Bradley was first off the mark. 'It's pretty clear what the Krauts were up to, Ken. And you've given me a piece of important information.' He pointed at the map. 'They're obviously heading for the southern part of the Meuse – providing they can break out of the Ardennes. They want the Huy, Dinant and perhaps Liège bridges so that they can do another gallop through Belgium into Northern France.'

'Like in 1940,' Ike commented.

'Yes, but this is 1944 and they'll never get within sight of those goddam bridges.'

Strong waited until the others had studied

the map and had absorbed Bradley's explanation. 'You might well be right, General,' he said. 'They could have been scouts, feeling out the situation at the bridges. But there is one more thing.' He paused and pulled out a photograph which Betts had given him. 'With the money on the dead men in the jeep, the British tank unit found this.' He passed the photograph to Eisenhower. 'You can see, General, that you figure prominently on it.' He turned to Bradley. 'And you too.'

The generals crowded round to get a look over Eisenhower's shoulder.

The Supreme Commander's brow creased. 'That must have been taken in Granville – at my HQ in the Villa Montgomery – when I was crocked with my lousy football knee, and you,' he nodded to Bradley, 'and Monty and Patton came down to see me to discuss the Aachen situation, some time last September. But what the hell have they done to our heads?'

Strong took the photo from him and studied it for a moment. A circle had been drawn around each of the four heads on the US Signal Corps photograph, with each circle cut by crosslines meeting in the centre of the face. He gave a shudder of apprehension. Then he dismissed the thought; it was too impossible. He put the photograph back with the rest of the papers. 'I … I don't really know, sir.'

III

'THIS IS YOUR ROAD TO THE FUTURE,' the sign read. 'BY COURTESY OF THE 82ND ENGINEER BATTALION, US ARMY.'

But if the little Luxembourg road along which the Sherman crawled in the long tail-to-tail convoy escaping from the front led to the future, it was a future that was crazy, bizarre, frightening. They passed a dead cow in a field, its legs protruding rigidly from its bloated body making it look like a tethered balloon, an abandoned tank destroyer, with one track stretched behind it like a broken limb, an ambulance smashed into a ditch, one side of the windscreen shattered like cracked ice, the dead it had been carrying sprawled grotesquely in the snow.

Gerling, standing in the turret next to Hartmann, took in the scene as they approached the village which was their first objective. The Americans were clearly 'bugging out', as they called it. They passed a desert battery of field guns, muzzles pointing expectantly skywards, neat piles of shells near each piece, but there were no crews to serve them. All that was left of the village's defensive force were two Americans in tight long black raincoats, squatting in a ditch near a dug-in anti-tank gun, their faces pale, bearded and lost. They did not look up as the Sherman rumbled by.

They passed some half-timbered, white-painted houses with their windows tightly shuttered. Hartmann snapped a command through the throat mike and Maier, in the driver's seat, pulled the thirty-ton vehicle out of the convoy which they had joined three hours before. Rolling into the centre of the village, its shops and houses showing no sign of life, they came into a square full of American troops, tankers and infantry. It was a confused mess of half a hundred different outfits.

Hartmann nudged Gerling as Maier brought the Sherman to a stop. 'Look at that,' he whispered. 'They've had it, haven't they?'

Gerling did not answer, but the sergeant was right. Defeat was in the very air.

Many of the Americans were totally worn out, squatting in the snow, heads sunk between their knees, too weary even to accept the hot food that a group was cooking over a fire made from doors and fixtures they had ripped from a nearby house. Others stood round the fire staring blankly ahead, apathetic to the officers pacing nervously back and forth, discussing the situation in low voices. Most of them had thrown away their weapons a long time ago.

An officer got out of a mud-splattered jeep, and looked at the apathetic faces of the men, waiting to be taken prisoner. He grabbed an abandoned 30-inch carbine and strode back the way he had come. 'No gas,' he snapped as he came level with the Sherman, 'wanna come along?' He indicated the front behind them. Hartmann shook his head wordlessly.

The young officer spat in the gutter. 'Another bunch o' yeller bellies like the rest, eh,' he snarled. He went on alone.

Hartmann waited till the young officer was out of earshot. 'All right, Gerling,' he said. 'You're in charge while I'm away.'

'Away?' Gerling queried, not attempting to conceal his dislike of the sergeant, which had been in no way diminished by Hartmann's total lack of communication about the purpose of their mission.

'Yes, away; our first V-man is here. He's got some information for us.'

'What kind of information?'

'We're running out of gas; he'll tell us where supplies can be found.'

'You mean the Organisation managed to bury a supply of gas in September before the *Amis* ran us out?'

Hartmann frowned. He didn't welcome references to Germany's defeats which he believed had been caused by the generals' treachery the previous July and by the Americans' technical preponderance. 'No, we didn't have time then.'

'Well, in that case the only place we're going to get gas is the nearest *Ami* POL depot.'

'I am well aware of that,' Hartmann said frigidly, 'but there is other information I need from our agent.'

'What?' Gerling persisted.

Hartmann pulled off his leather helmet and swung his leg over the turret. 'It is none of your business. I shall be back in fifteen minutes.' And with that he disappeared into the throng of Americans.

Sailor watched him go and then turned to Gerling. 'Can we brew up?' His accent was noticeably Irish.

'Okay, Sailor,' Gerling said, 'But don't get mixing with those *Amis*. With that accent of yours, you stick out like a sore thumb. If the *Amis* want to talk, leave it to Maier; he's got the right accent.'

'Wilco,' Maier said, pulling himself out of the driving hatch and looking at the crowd of beaten Americans.

Rapidly he and Sailor filled the blackened can at the back of the Sherman with sand from the sandbag. Sailor poured the rest of the gas from the jerrican into the sand and stirred the mixture with his bayonet to the consistency of thick porridge. 'Okay, Sailor, get ya head out of the way,' Maier commanded in his tough Brooklyn accent, 'unless ya wanna lose it.'

He struck a match and dropped it into the mixture which ignited with a whoosh. Sailor undid the spade on the side of the *Gruesome Twosome* and held it over the fire while Maier started to slice spam and lay the slices on the blade. Gerling got out the canteen cups and sprinkled powdered coffee into them. Five minutes later they were drinking black coffee and eating charred slices of greasy spam, helped down with iron-hard British compo biscuits. Sailor balanced a slice of spam on the edge of his combat-knife blade and indicated the Americans, filling the little square. 'They've had it for sure,' he said.

Across from them a soldier in a dirty combat blouse, open to the waist, had managed to lever a cobblestone free from the pavement with his combat knife. He flung it with all his strength at the nearest boarded-up store window. A fat woman in a black apron with great pendulous breasts came rushing out of the store, screaming furiously in the local German dialect of the area. The man who had thrown the stone pushed her in her fat red face with the flat of his hand and she landed in the mud with her legs in the air.

'Over here, fellers!' An unshaven private of the 106th Infantry Division shouted. 'These gooks have cognac here!'

There was a rush towards the little pub, the door giving way under the weight of a dozen heavy shoulders.

Maier looked at the others. 'My God,' he breathed, 'I never saw anything like this in Russia!'

Gerling nodded, but he was no longer concerned with the *Amis*. There was going to be trouble here – a lot of trouble and he wanted to be away before it started. But where the hell had Hartmann got to?

Then he spotted him, fighting his way through the crowd of soldiers busy fighting for the bottles which were being handed out from the looted pub. A PFC, already drunk, tried to press a drink on him. Hartmann kneed him in the groin and he sank to the ground, clutching his privates. Nobody seemed to notice as he disappeared beneath the feet of the screaming mob.

As he neared the Sherman, Hartmann formed his thumb and finger into a circle, the American sign of success. Obviously he had met his V-man.

'There's a POL depot two kilometres from here. Just before Esch.' Hartmann indicated the road running south out of the village. 'It's about five hundred metres from the main highway.'

'Defended?' Gerling asked.

'Half a company,' Hartmann said easily.

'*Half a company!*' Sailor whistled dismally through his pursed limps. 'That's a helluva lot for the four of us.'

Hartmann smiled contemptuously. He jerked his thumb at the drunken mob in the village square, not even deigning to turn. 'Against that rabble!' he said. 'Besides one look at the *Gruesome Twosome* and they'll piss their pants. After all they're only niggers.'

DAY TWO:
SUNDAY, 17 DECEMBER, 1944

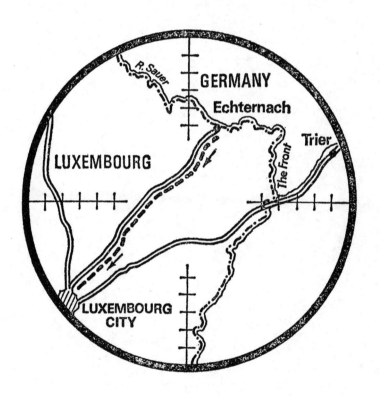

I

It was dawn. On the horizon the smoking factory chimneys of Esch-sur-Alzette, the industrial town which straddled the Franco-Luxembourg border, were already pumping smoke into the sky.

'I'll take the gun,' Hartmann said as they turned off the main road, following the sign which indicated the '37th POL DEPOT'. There was a sudden gleam in his blue eyes, as if he were remembering other times and other things. Gerling moved to one side in the narrow confines of the turret. Hartmann pulled back the breech lever. He took one of the long 75-mm shells from the rack and rammed it home. 'Just in case,' he said, bending down to adjust the rubber-capped telescopic sight.

As they rattled on, the sky began to turn a leaden white. Gerling was sure it was going to snow and the Sherman would be a bitch to drive in snow. Unlike the Tiger, which Maier was used to, it did not have the wide snow tracks that had been essential on the Eastern front.

'There it is,' Maier's voice crackled over the headphones. Gerling thrust his head above the turret. The wind was icy and his eyes began to water.

'Slow down.'

It was the 37th POL Depot all right – a muddy couple of acres of countryside, surrounded by barbed wire and filled with drum after drum of oil and petrol for the troops at the front, with five dreary olive-drab winterised squad huts for the Service of Supply men who ran the place.

They rolled closer. The big gate with the large 'KEEP OUT' and 'NO SMOKING: POL' signs was closed, and there was a guard – a tall coloured soldier, a carbine slung over his shoulder – standing by it shivering in the cold.

As they came to a halt, he looked up at Gerling and asked in a thick southern accent, 'What do you want, soldier?'

'We're running out of gas,' Gerling said in his best American accent. 'We'd kinda like to fill up here.'

'Got orders?' the guard asked.

'Sure,' he said and handed down the papers which had been prepared for them so carefully at Grafenwoehr.

The guard looked at them and then handed them back. Maier let out the clutch and the Sherman started forward. But the Negro wasn't through with them yet. He held up his hand, as if he were a traffic policeman. 'Hold it,' he said, 'you ain't given

40

me the password.'

Gerling pulled a face. 'Password! Hell, soldier, you heard the radio this morning? Everybody's bugging out at the front. The Krauts are coming. Jesus H., how would I know the password!'

The Negro unslung his carbine slowly. 'No password – no gas, soldier. Them's my orders and I'm sticking to them.' Uncertainly but still determined, he levelled the carbine at Gerling.

Hartmann pushed Gerling to one side in the turret. 'Listen, you,' he snapped, 'I want gas – and I want it fast, get that!'

'But darn it, sarge,' he protested, 'I've got my orders.'

Hartmann put his hand on the square butt of his forty-five. 'I don't want any of your lip, boy. I want in!'

The young guard's jaw tightened. Gerling could see his skinny brown finger curl around the trigger of the carbine. 'But you gotta have the password.'

Hartmann ignored him. He touched his throat mike. 'Roll 'em,' he ordered Maier.

The Sherman started to move forward again. The guard raised his carbine, hesitation mirrored in his face, his eyes wide and white with fear. 'I'll fire, if you guys don't stop!' he shouted above the roar of the Sherman's engines.

Hartmann did not give him a chance. He

drew and fired at the same moment. The Negro's face disappeared in a mess of red gore and he slumped down beside the fence.

Next moment the tank hit the wire. The posts held for an instant, then buckled. The Sherman ground on in bottom gear, ripping the wire apart and pulling shreds of it behind it. Hartmann slipped back into the gunner's seat.

The pistol shot and roar of the tank's 340 HP engine woke the camp. Suddenly all was noise, orders, screams. A group of night-shift workers loading oil barrels on to a truck dropped what they were doing and ran for the shelter of the huts. Lights clicked on in spite of the blackout.

Hartmann pressed the button of the forward 30-inch machine gun. A stream of lead – every third slug a red tracer – stitched the air. The first bunch of men trying to get out of the nearest hut went down.

He swung the gun fast. A big Negro, aided by an undersized corporal, was fumbling with an anti-tank bazooka in the corner of the muddy square. The burst caught them, just as they were fitting the rocket. They went down screaming.

A big Negro sergeant ran towards them shouting, a tommy gun tucked into his hip. He was hit before he got ten yards. Sprawled full length in the mud, the Sherman rolled over him.

Gerling ducked as a patter of slugs struck the Sherman. While a group of men behind the second hut covered him, a young Negro in long white underwear was running desperately for the abandoned truck.

Hartmann fired a long burst at the second hut and the small arms fire stopped. He swung round, and fired again. Gerling could see the mud spurt up at the running man's feet. Hartmann had missed!

The Negro flung himself into the truck and feverishly tried to get it started. He threw a quick glance at Hartmann who was grinning, his eyes gleaming with the *Blutrausch*. Pressing his face against the sight, Hartmann pulled the firing lever.

The Sherman shuddered. Gerling opened his mouth to prevent his eardrums bursting, as an acrid, cordite-laden blast slapped him in the face. The breech came racing back and the empty cartridge case tumbled to the floor. Pressing the fume extractor button, he stared out of the periscope. The truck had sagged down at the back, its axle broken and thick black smoke was pouring from it. A moment later the gas tank exploded and the truck vanished.

The destruction seemed to act as a signal for Hartmann. His eyes gleaming, he pumped shell after shell at the huts, destroying them one after the other. While the fume extractor roared in its attempt to clear the turret, he let go of the 75-mm and seized the 50-mm gun on the turret's lip. Clasping both handles, he swung it left and right, pouring four hundred rounds a minute into the terrified Negroes, cutting great swathes in their ranks as they huddled next to the shattered huts.

Gerling stared at him in horror. This was sheer massacre.

'*Hartmann!*' he yelled above the chatter of the gun and the screams of the wounded and dying Negroes piling up against the huts. 'Hartmann, for God's sake, stop it!'

But Hartmann kept on firing, the sweat pouring down his face.

'*Stop it!*'

'They're scum, *Ami* scum,' Hartmann yelled, 'they deserve to die.'

Gerling hesitated no longer. He slapped the other man hard across the face. 'Hartmann!' he roared at the top of his voice.

Hartmann let go of the gun and blinked as if he were coming out of a trance. 'We've got to get the gas and get the hell out of here. All the *Amis* in Esch will be heading down here in a few minutes,' shouted Gerling.

'Yes, yes,' Hartmann stuttered, a glazed look in his eyes, his body suddenly limp and without strength. To Gerling he looked like a man who had just screwed a woman. But he had no time to consider the pheno-menon. They had to get the gas – and quick.

'Okay Maier – head for that pump. You, Sailor, get up top and help him. Hartmann, you keep watch on the survivors.' He indicated the groaning handful of seriously wounded men who had survived the massacre.

Fifteen minutes later they were rolling along a dirt road towards the slag heaps which marked the French border, while the sirens of Esch sounded their urgent warning. Gerling, drained of emotion, sat slumped in the commander's seat. For the first time he realised just what he had got himself into when he had volunteered for *Unternehmen Greif* six weeks before.

II

It had all started innocently enough at the *Nummer III Feldlazarett* in the ancient university town of Heidelberg where he had been recovering from his third wound.

The *Chefarzt*, a kindly man for an Army doctor, had stopped during his morning rounds and opened the door to the little white-painted room he shared with the 'lower stomach', as the nurses called his unconscious fellow patient. 'How's he been during the night?' He indicated the young officer who had been struck in the abdomen with a solid-shot armour piercing shell during the fighting in Poland.

Gerling shrugged and then regretted it. His shoulder still hurt like hell. 'Nothing to report, Herr Doktor,' he said and wrinkled his nose. 'Except the smell. It's pretty awful this morning.'

The doctor grinned. 'To me it smells like attar of roses. I've spent half the night messing around in you fellows' shit, trying to discover which of you veterans of the great German victory in Russia have brought home some nice cases of amoebic dysentery – as well as syph.'

Gerling liked the doctor. He was always complaining about his military patients and Gerling knew that he only kept himself going, trying to meet the demands of the hopelessly overcrowded military hospital, by drugging himself with *preludin*.

'Syph, *Herr Doktor?*' he said. 'I haven't had it for so long I've almost forgotten how to get it.'

'Don't worry, wait till some of those pretty *Blitzmadchen* down at headquarters get a look at your handsome mug and that nice SS uniform of yours. And all those decorations! What chance does a poor rear-line stallion like me have with the likes of you around?'

Gerling changed the subject. 'Got anything for the patient to drink today, *Herr Doktor?* I missed my medicine last night. It helps me to forget the stink.'

The doctor closed the door behind him and pulled a small bottle of *Korn* from beneath his apron. 'Here you are and God help your liver. Oh, yes, and I've got something else for you.' He rummaged in the big pocket in the front of his apron and brought out a yellow piece of paper. 'Top secret, as you can see. Came in at six this morning. By seven o'clock every damned orderly in the place knew what it contained. Excellent security, eh?'

He bent over Gerling, the banter absent now. 'Have a look at it, while I examine your arm.'

Gerling held the paper in his right hand while the *Chefarzt* looked at his shoulder where an explosive bullet had taken a chunk out of it. The message read:

'To all units of the *Wehrmacht*, Navy and Air Force – and *Waffen SS*, with the exception of the fortresses on the Atlantic.

The Fuehrer has ordered the formation of special troops for employment in reconnaissance in the west, strength approx 2 battalions.

All captured US uniforms, equipment and vehicles are to be surrendered to the Quartermaster-General's Office by all formations, including *Waffen SS*. Volunteers are asked for from all formations. They must:

(a) Be physically fit for special duties, intelligent and agile.
(b) Fully combat trained.
(c) Have a knowledge of English, especially the American dialect, and understand military terms in these tongues.

This order is to be made to all units at once. Volunteers are to report to *Oberstuermbannfuehrer* Skorzeny at Friedenthal near Berlin.
Signed KEITEL.'

'Skorzeny, that's the fellow who rescued Mussolini last year, isn't it?' Gerling asked, and winced as the doctor touched a nerve.
'Yes. But don't take that too seriously,' the doctor answered. 'Those days are over. To my way of thinking it could be a nice cushy billet for you. You speak fluent English, don't you?'
'What do you mean?'
'Well, it can't be that secret if we get a copy as a routine message. My guess is that they're looking for linguists to man listening posts at the front, tuned in to Allied radio traffic.'
Gerling stared out at the wooded heights of the *Odenwald*. Heavy rain clouds hung

above them. Soon it would be raining again; it always seemed to rain in Heidelberg. If the war ever came to an end, he thought to himself, and he managed to get to a university, it would not be the University of Heidelberg. 'Oh, I don't know, *Herr Doktor,*' he said after a few moments. 'I think I'd prefer to go back to the *Leibstandarte,* or what's left of it.' His face fell, as he thought of the casualties of the previous summer's fighting. There were very few of the officers left who had started the war with him.

The doctor shook his head. 'Can't you get enough of it, young man?' He pointed to the ugly hole in the stomach wall, the series of neat holes across his left breast above the nipple which looked as if they had been stitched by a sewing machine, the shoulder wound, still pink and ugly, although it was healing well enough. '*Stuermbannfuehrer* Gerling, you are a glutton for punishment.'

He cast a quick glance towards the window to make sure that no one was on the balcony outside. Gerling knew the look. In the Army they called it contemptuously the 'German look' – the look Germans gave in 1944 when they wanted to impart some information which might land them in a Gestapo cellar.

'Let's face it, Gerling,' he said, after the brief security check, 'we've lost this war. The *Amis* are in the Eifel and the *Ivans* [the

Russians] are in Poland. It can only be a few weeks, a couple of months at the most before the whole bloody rotten mess is over. Why risk your neck any more? You've done your bit.'

Gerling wriggled in his bed. He remembered how the division had rolled into Russia in July, 1941. Nearly sixteen thousand of them, young, vigorous, confident, full of belief in the cause, the elite of the *Waffen SS*, Germany's premier division. That winter the division had withered away. When it was finally pulled out for refitting, regiments were down to company strength and companies to that of platoons.

In '42 they had been re-equipped and refilled with more young men eager to die for the glory of a Greater Germany – which they did in their thousands. Four months later they were withdrawn for the next refitting. This time the faces were strange – those of young 'volunteers' from all over Occupied Europe, drawn to the *Waffen SS* recruiting offices by the lies about a 'New Europe' united in the fight against the 'Bolshevik menace'. It had happened time and time again, interrupted only by that terrible journey in the freezing, straw-filled goods train, packed with the wounded, their bodies lousy with lice. Then the *Lazarett*, where the tired surgeons in gumboots and bloody aprons, sawing, cutting, hacking, had no time save for one harsh instruction to hollow-eyed Red Cross sisters, 'Amputate!'

He looked up at the doctor, whose two sons had been killed at Stalingrad, and said slowly. 'Yes, *Herr Chefarzt,* I think I will have a look at it.'

He passed the initial English language test with flying colours. He was the only one of the thirty hopefuls who could pronounce 'Swiss cheese' and 'Vera veered wildly to Perivale' to the satisfaction of the Professor of English from Hamburg University who acted as their examiner.

But why shouldn't he? His mother had always insisted they should speak English at home, in spite of his father, the general's, good-humoured protests about that 'damned English sing-song at the coffee table'. And each summer he had spent several months in England, the England which his mother had loved so much and which had killed her in July, 1943, when the RAF launched its great raid on Hamburg. Indirectly it had caused his father's death too. He had not been able to get over his wife's death and, although years overage, had volunteered for an administrative job in the quartermaster branch, only to be killed four months later when the partisans raided his HQ in Minsk.

Two days later he received his marching orders. The *Chefarzt* hugged him with untypical demonstrativeness. 'Look after yourself, my boy,' he said and there were real tears in his eyes. 'Remember,' he ended with a trace of his old cynicism, 'the Greater German Reich will have need of young men like you in the difficult years to come.'

His journey to Grafenwoehr in Bavaria was long and somewhat mysterious. The rest of the troop train was packed with cursing sweating *Landsers* on the way back to the Italian front, but his coach was virtually empty when they left Heidelberg. Gradually it began to fill up with a strangely assorted bunch of men from all arms of the service – *Luftwaffe, Waffen SS, Kriegsmarine*, even the Merchant Navy. Time and again it would stop at some one-horse station and the train commandant would shout out, 'Special Commando for Rappenberg' (the station nearest to Grafenwoehr), and an odd soldier, in every case his chest covered with medals, would grab his pack and enter the long coach.

At last they descended at the little Bavarian station, thirty or so of them, standing there in the chill gloom. A captain in the *Kriegsmarine*, a typical seadog with the silver of the Naval Destroyer's badge on his chest, took over. In a voice thickened by *Korn* and shouting orders against the wind, he bellowed 'Fall in!' Awkwardly because of their varying ranks, ranging from major in the SS to corporal in the Luftwaffe, they formed up while the naval captain strode off to the RTO's office.

Gerling cast a glance at the men lined up with him. They didn't exactly look like men who had been picked for some cushy listening job with military intelligence. Most of them wore the silver wound medal indicating that they had been wounded three times and every one of them bore the silver or gilt bars of the close combat award or the tank assault badges. There was something about their faces which indicated that these men were the survivors, fighting men who had fought from the very start on every front from the Desert to Norway, from the Channel to Moscow and had survived because they had been tougher and smarter than the rest.

'What do you make of it, comrade?'

He turned to the man on his left, a tall *Oberstuermbannfuehrer* with a thin face and the Knight's Cross at his throat. The arm-band round his sleeve indicated he was from the *Reich SS Panzer Division*.

'Gerling, *Leibstandarte*,' he introduced himself quickly. The other man was one grade higher than he, but that did not mean much in the easy camaraderie of the *Waffen SS*, where the men sometimes addressed their officers in the familiar 'thou' form. 'I'm not quite sure, comrade. But I have an awful feeling that I've volunteered for the wrong outfit.'

'Yeah, you might get "a sore throat" at last on this one, *Stuermbannfuehrer*,' a voice behind him said. Gerling turned. A cheeky pair of blue eyes stared at him, from a tough brown face.

'*Obermaat* Smith,' the man wearing the navy-blue pea-jacket of the Kriegsmarine introduced himself. 'I'm a bastard,' he added airily, 'half-Irish, half-English and one hundred per cent Kraut.'

Gerling laughed. He knew what the cocky petty officer meant by a 'sore throat'. He touched his neck and said, 'I've no ambitions to get the Knight's Cross, thank you, *Obermaat*.'

He turned back to the *Oberstuermbannfuehrer*, who now introduced himself briefly as 'Hartmann'. 'You an English linguist too?' he asked, trying to make conversation.

'Yes, I have the great misfortune of knowing the American dialect. My mother...'

His explanation was interrupted by the naval captain's hoarse voice. 'All right, all of you, listen to this.' He nodded to the immaculate SS captain who had emerged from the RTO's office with him.

Without any preliminaries, the SS captain said 'You are now members of the 150th Panzer Brigade, which is a completely independent unit attached to no division. From

54

this moment onwards you must observe the strictest secrecy. No letters to your relatives. No attempt to communicate with anyone else outside the camp at Grafenwoehr. Nor will you impart any information you may learn there to anyone else outside the team to which you will be assigned, is that understood?' He paused momentarily to let the information sink in. 'Any breach of security will be punished by death.'

There was the loud obscene sound of someone breaking wind. It was *Obermaat* Smith.

'Excuse me, sir,' Smith said politely. 'It just slipped out. Please carry on.'

The captain's lower lip trembled, but he preserved his self-control. 'All right, you will now come forward one by one and hand in your identity cards and march orders, plus all other documents you may have in your possession.'

Obediently they shuffled forward to where the SS captain stood, now supported by two huge 'chain dogs' – hard-faced military policemen, identified by the silver plate hanging from a chain round their necks – examining each document carefully with his flashlight.

'You are Maier?' the SS captain flashed his torch in the face of a small Panzer corporal just ahead of Gerling.

'*Jawohl, Herr Hauptmann.*'

The SS captain stared hard at the man's ID card. 'You are a driver, I see?'

'Yes sir.'

'Good, our driver has got drunk while we have been waiting for you. You will take his place. *Verstanden?*'

'Yes sir.'

An hour later after a confusing ride over the dirt roads of the Bavarian hinterland, they came to the camp – a series of wooden huts, surrounded by a triple, high-wire fence with towers at each corner. There was no light save the four searchlights playing over the darkened huts and the dim blue lantern hanging over the gate.

'Shit on a Christmas tree!' Smith exclaimed from the back of the truck, as they braked to a halt. 'Isn't this just a home from home.'

One by one they dropped to the frozen earth and stared curiously at the darkened camp and the dozen SS guards, with swarthy un-German faces who had appeared out of the gloom, sub-machines slung over their chests, Alsatian dogs restrained by the chains they held in their hands.

'Nice little lap-dogs you've got there, comrades,' Smith quipped to the nearest guard.

The SS man grunted something, but Smith was not put off. 'Where the hell is this place, comrade?' He stepped forward.

The guard snapped something in a Slavic tongue, and the dog leapt forward. At the very last moment, the guard caught it. There was the snap of the chain as the Alsatian was stopped in mid-air, its snout a few inches from Smith's face.

The SS man grinned evilly. '*Nix sprechen, Kamerad*,' he cautioned in broken German.

Smith got back into the group hurriedly. 'Not what you call a warm welcome, is it?' he said a little shakily and forced a laugh.

But no one laughed with him.

For the next few weeks the pace in the strange Bavarian camp was hectic. The *Kommandokompanie*, to which the thirty new arrivals were assigned, was obviously intended for something more than listening to enemy radio traffic – that was immediately clear. Admittedly every morning they were shown captured American Signal Corps films and Hollywood war movies and were given regular language instruction in order to familiarise themselves with American military jargon. But afternoons were devoted to intensive unarmed combat, training with silenced US 45 colts and the use of the AFU radio transmitter, which Gerling knew could only be intended for one thing – clandestine operations.

As November gave way to December, they were called to the quartermaster's store and confronted with a huge heap of olive-drab clothing that reached up to the beamed roof. All the various bits of uniform were cleanly washed, but there was a smell of death about them and there were suspicious dark patches on some of the jackets. Stuka, the enormously fat quartermaster-sergeant, beamed at their surprised looks. 'Yes gentlemen,' he said, '*Ami* uniforms, all tailored in best quality material.' He picked up an 'Eisenhower jacket', and ran it through his fat fingers. 'You can't get material like that in Germany these days. Genuine one hundred per cent wool,' he said proudly, as if the fact was to his own credit.

'Surprised you ain't flogged it down town,' Smith quipped.

'I wouldn't do that, *Obermaat*,' he said jovially. 'How would you keep your big arse warm out there if I did.' He did not explain what he meant by 'out there'.

'All right, gentlemen, we didn't have time to find any Yid tailors in the camps to take your measurements, so you'll have to find uniforms to fit you as best you can.'

The next morning, outfitted in *Ami* uniforms with ranks which bore no relation to their real ranks, they started what their German-American instructor told them cynically was 'ya deportment drill'. 'I wanna see you guys relax. Do ya understand, *relax*,' he announced. 'We ain't in the *Leibstandarte* now. We're in the freedom-loving, democratic United States Army, and Uncle Sugar likes his soldiers to relax.'

All that day they played at 'relaxing'. Time and again the cynical German-American sergeant would say wearily, 'For God's sake, wise up! Let's see you chew that gum. Roll it from side to side. And for Chrissake, walk from the hips, roll 'em. Let's see ya butts move.'

Smith grunted, 'Hell's bells, I feel like an "auntie" on the *Reeperbahn*, looking for a sailor for a bit of the other.'

The uniforms and the arrival of Shermans, battered patched-up American tanks captured in the fighting of the previous autumn, helped to increase the rumours with which the strange training camp seethed. At night in their dormitories with the green-tiled Bavarian ovens crackling in the corner and the only sound the steady tread of the Ukrainian SS guards outside, patrolling the searchlight-swept grounds, they passed the latest 'latrine-gram' from mouth to mouth in whispered apprehension. They were going to break through the *Ami* lines and try to reach the German-held fortresses on the Atlantic, besieged and cut off from the Homeland since the summer. They were to attempt to break into the only big city held by the *Amis*, the Imperial City of Aachen and 'liquidate' all the traitors there who had collaborated with the enemy, as a warning to the rest of the threatened Rhineland. They were to break into the huge *Ami* POW cages near Cherbourg, release the thousands of prisoners held there and with them start a revolt behind the Allied lines, thus taking the pressure off the Rhineland.

One day in that first week of December they finally learned the code-name of the operation in which they were to take part. It was ambiguous like everything else in that strange camp. It could mean Operation 'Grab' or 'Gryphon', that mythical bird of the old legends. One young *Luftwaffe* officer took it to mean the former, as he explained in the hushed silence of the dormitory. 'We're to break through the *Ami* lines in little groups – at most four or five of us in one vehicle, that's why the tanks are there. We'll rendezvous at the Café de la Paix just near the Opera House. That'll be our headquarters for "Operation Grab"!' he concluded proudly.

'But who or what are we going to grab?'

'It's obvious,' he exclaimed. 'There's only one guy worth all the fuss and expense of our training – *the Supreme Commander himself, Eisenhower!*'

Two days after the Eisenhower rumour had swept through the camp, they were ordered to break up into small teams, just as the *Luftwaffe* lieutenant had said they would be.

60

There were two types – 'Ford Distance Teams', six men, driving Ford trucks, and 'Long Range Distance Teams', made up of four men, equipped with captured US jeeps.

Gerling found himself in one of the 'Long Range Distance Teams' with Maier, the pale-faced tanker, *Obermaat* Smith, whom everyone now called 'Sailor' because of his rolling walk and big Hamburg waterfront mouth which had no respect for anyone, and the thin-faced bearer of the Knight's Cross who had introduced himself on the first day at the little railway station as Hartmann.

Gerling got on with the two enlisted men right from the start, but Hartmann was different. At first he thought it was the difference in rank or the fact that Hartmann had won Germany's highest decoration for bravery, but after he had spent a day with him in the US POW camp at Mooseberg, mixing with US prisoners in order to familiarise themselves with American ways (Hartmann spoke flawless American English), Gerling realised that it was something else. Hartmann's virulent hatred was almost pathological, balanced as it was by a blind devotion to the National Socialist cause.

After they had left the camp, squatting face to face in the back of the coal-driven *Wehrmacht* truck which had come to fetch them back to Grafenwoehr, he could not conceal his utter contempt of the Americans.

'Aren't they just scum,' he said in disgust, almost as soon as the great barbed wire gate closed behind them. He tore off his khaki stocking cap and ripped open the dirty GI blouse as if to exemplify his hatred of the *Amis*.

Gerling shrugged. 'POWs never look very good. The shock of capture, the rations, the breakdown of military discipline. In five years I've seen a lot of prisoners from all over Europe. They all look much the same to me.'

Hartmann spat out of the back of the truck. 'No self-respecting German soldier would let himself go like that,' he said firmly. 'Did they look like soldiers? Hands in their pockets, unshaven, clothes filthy! They're all damn cowboys, little Jewboy shopkeepers, bandits. All of them – they're degenerates; they lack moral fibre.'

Gerling looked at Hartmann. The man's vehemence shocked him. 'Do you think so?' he asked. 'They don't seem to be doing too badly at the moment.'

Hartmann's lips twisted in scorn. 'No wonder, with their overwhelming technical resources. We put a man out in a field with a m.g. 42 and they send half their air force plus an artillery group to get rid of him before their infantry dare advance again. They're scared. Believe you me, they're cowards – all of them. I know the *Amis*. I lived in the damned country for twelve years. After all my father was an American, you know.'

Four days before they were due to leave the camp for their start position in the faraway Eifel, the commander of the 150 Panzer Brigade, the legendary *Oberstuermbann-fuehrer* Otto Skorzeny, head of the Security Service's sabotage and subversion service, came to see his men for the first time.

The man who had rescued Mussolini from his eagle-top mountain prison and kidnapped Admiral Horthy's son in order to force the Hungarian dictator to stay in the war on Germany's side was even bigger than Gerling had expected him to be from the photos in the *Voelkischer Beobachter*. He towered head and shoulders above his two SS adjutants as he swaggered to the rostrum in the centre of the square, his breast gleaming with medals and orders, a faint smile on his sabre-slashed face, the result of his student duelling days in Vienna.

'*Guten Morgen, Soldaten!*' he rapped out the traditional military greeting. Gerling smiled slightly at the Austrian's attempt to be more Prussian than the Prussians. With a big grin on his sallow face, he said in pure Viennese, 'You look a fine bunch of *Amis*, standing there with your fingers stuck down at your sides like a regiment of Prussian grenadiers. *Relax!* And that's an order.'

There were a few soft chuckles and the muted shuffle of their rubber-soled American boots as they 'relaxed'.

Skorzeny waited a moment then continued. 'Soldiers, you are my élite. All of you are experienced soldiers – and more. You are now skilled saboteurs and speak the language of the American enemy expertly. Out of the three thousand odd soldiers of my brigade, you are the best.'

He paused and looked along their ranks. 'Here's the catch,' Sailor whispered softly to Gerling. 'First they build you up and then they get you by the short and curlies.'

'And because you are the best, the Fuehrer has ordered me to pick you for a special task. The bulk of my brigade will have the job of leading a great new offensive in the west, which will throw the Anglo-Americans back from our frontiers. We shall attack the Americans through the Ardennes and it will be the mission of my brigade to capture the vital bridges across the River Meuse between Liège and Dinant. You, however, are being reserved for an even more vital mission, so vital that I cannot tell you in a group what exactly this mission will be. According to Fuehrer Order Number One of 1940, each man will only know enough of the mission to be able to carry it out successfully. This order applies to you.'

He turned to his adjutant, Baron von Foelkersam. '*Stuermbannfuehrer* von Foelkersam and I will brief each individual team leader on his part of the mission. I have given a lot of thought to your mission over these last weeks. Each and every one of you will enter the enemy lines, wearing enemy uniform. You know what that will mean if you are captured. You are naturally all brave men who have proved yourselves time and again in the bloody fighting of these last years; that I know. For that reason let us keep secret our individual tasks, even from the other men in the same team. Thus no offer of freedom by the enemy could induce any man to betray the others' missions.'

His sentence trailed away to nothing, as if, for the first time, he was realising the full impact of his words. Then he shook himself out of his reverie. His heels clicked together, and his arm shot out in the German greeting. '*Soldaten,*' he bellowed at the top of his voice, '*Sieg Heil!*'

III

While the *Gruesome Twosome* ground on up the steep slope that led from Aumetz to their next rendezvous with Hartmann's mysterious V-men, General George Patton at his

HQ in Nancy was still fuming because Bradley had ordered his 10th Armored Division to the Ardennes. Patton, who had the best fighting reputation of any general officer in 12th Army Group, called up General Eddy, the commander of the corps to which the 4th Armored Division belonged. Let Brad take the 10th, but he certainly wasn't getting his élite 4th, the spearhead of all his spectacular advances in these last few months. 'Listen, Matt, engage the 4th Armored fast. I don't want to lose them too, understand?'

Eddy sighed. He was used to his chief's unpredictable changes of plans, and he didn't protest. Patton would relieve a corps commander at the slightest hesitation. 'Will do, George,' he said morosely.

While Patton was on the telephone, the 10th Armored Division was moving through the cobbled back streets of the Luxembourg capital, driving past silent shuttered houses from which the flags and portraits of the Grand Duchess, Churchill and Roosevelt had been hastily removed, now that the Germans were coming back. While his division headed north, its commander, Major-General William Morris Jr, strode into the headquarters of 'Tubby' Barton, whose 4th Infantry Division was reeling back under the German attack at Echternach.

Barton, a battle-experienced soldier, but now sick and worried, flung his arms round

66

the surprised Morris. 'Thank God, you're here!' he exclaimed.

Morris backed off. For the first time since he had left the 3rd Army area he realised just how serious the situation was in the Ardennes. Bradley, returning from Versailles to his headquarters in the capital at that same moment had realised earlier that day just how bad the situation was. Three hours ago he had detoured to his advanced HQ at Verdun. His men there had been in a state of panic. *Maginot Casenne*, which housed the HQ, was seething with rumours. Already the MP posts on the French border were beginning to pick up deserters from VIII Corps in the Ardennes who had fled over fifty miles in a single day. Now the Provost Branch reported that the Krauts had dropped paratroopers behind the American lines and he had been forced to accept the services of a machine-gun jeep to escort his staff car the rest of the way back to Luxembourg.

As he crossed the border, Bradley spotted a modest stone cottage, where the loyal Luxembourger had hoisted an enormous Stars and Stripes. 'I hope he doesn't have to take that down,' he joked to Hansen, his aide.

'You mean we'll stay put in Luxembourg?'

'You can bet your life we will. I'm not going to budge this CP. It would scare everyone else to death.'

But when General Bradley finally got out of his staff car and walked to his advance TAC HQ in the State Railway Building in Luxembourg's main street, his mood of defiance had vanished. The faces of his staff officers grouped around the huge wall map were grim, as junior officers marked up more and more German formations on it. Bradley looked at the map in dismay. 'Lev,' he said to his Chief-of-Staff, 'just where has this son of a bitch gotten all his strength?'

'I don't know,' the other officer replied, 'but we've certainly got our hands full of Krauts.'

The two men moved a little way away from the rest of the staff officers and discussed the situation in hushed voices, but they did not get far in their discussion. 'General.' It was Hansen.

'Yeah,' Bradley snapped.

'General Hodges is on the phone from Spa.'

'Bradley,' he said, 'Listen, I was just about to call you, Courtney. I've got good news for you at last.'

Ever since dawn had brought the information about the full impact of the German counterattack, the courtly white-haired commander of the 1st US Army, had been pleading with Bradley over the phone for the two US airborne divisions which were Eisenhower's only reserves on the Continent.

'Yes,' Bradley continued, 'Ike has just released the 101st and 82nd Airborne. Where do you want them?'

Courney Hodges' sigh of relief was clearly audible over the scrambler. He thought for a moment. Already the Germans had surrounded the rail and road-head at St Vith and were advancing on his HQ at Spa; their guns were clearly audible. Soon they'd be making for the next major road and rail-head on their drive to the River Meuse. Bastogne. 'I want one at Bastogne and one thirty miles north at Werbomont,' he said. 'And the sooner the better!'

Fifty miles away from Luxembourg City that night, the *Gruesome Twosome* rumbled on towards its destination, its strangely assorted crew unaware that their commander had the task of disrupting that plan: four of them against a whole American Army.

DAY THREE:
MONDAY, 18 DECEMBER, 1944

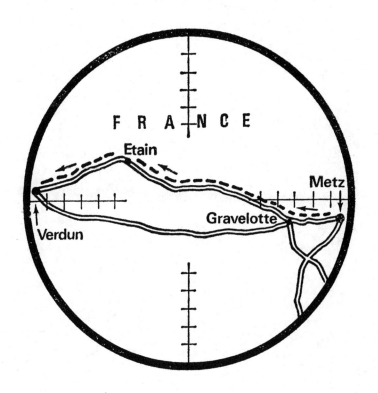

I

'Sarge,' Sailor said conversationally, shovelling another lump of hash into his mouth with the point of his combat knife, 'where the hell are we going?'

The Sherman was drawn up in a little cutting in the third class road that led from Aumetz to Metz, somewhere beyond the next ridge. 'The offensive's to the north.' He indicated the direction of the heavies' rumble, the ever-present background music of the war. 'Why are we moving south then? Hell, Sarge, we ain't even seen an *Ami* in the last hour or so.' He stuck another piece of the looted hash on the end of his knife.

Maier, crouching at the other side of the *Gruesome Twosome*, warming his hands on a cup of coffee looked at Hartmann expectantly.

'*Oberstuermbannfuehrer* Skorzeny told you that only the leader of the mission would know what it's about.' He stared at each of them in turn. 'There could be a traitor among you,' he said slowly.

Gerling looked at him in amazement. But the man was deadly serious. Sailor broke the heavy silence with a chuckle. 'Come off it,

Sarge,' he said. 'A traitor among us, the élite of the German Army! Each one of us a firm believer in the victory of the Greater German Reich,' he added cynically.

Hartmann looked at him coldly. 'One day, Smith, that loose tongue of yours will get you into serious trouble.'

Smith's face lost its grin but he did not take his eyes from Hartmann's face.

Then Hartmann seemed to make up his mind. 'Let me say this to you,' he said. 'Our most immediate task is to get into Metz this evening and obtain some information from one of our V-men. As to our final mission, this much I can tell you. We are going to kill someone – *someone very important*. I know that much, but who he is, well our contact in Metz will tell us that.'

With sirens howling the little procession of White scout cars, followed by the gleaming staff car, roared at full speed through Nancy's Place Stanislas. Standing upright in the staff car, as if he were some Roman Emperor in a chariot, General George Patton nodded imperiously to the shabby French civilians who whipped off their berets when they saw him. But the scowl on his face, under the gleaming lacquered helmet with its oversized silver stars, did not relax this morning as he swept through the town on his way to his HQ in the barracks at the Rue

74

du Sergent Blandau.

On this morning, with the new counter-offensive two days old and the whole of France trembling in fear that the Boche were coming back, the general was determined to show the flag, to remind them that he at least, *le Général Patton,* was here to protect them from the machinations of the enemy.

The little convoy rolled into the barracks which housed 3rd Army's HQ. The guards on the gate snapped to attention and Patton checked to see that they were wearing their neckties. He did not tolerate the slackness of the 1st and 7th Armies in his command even in a combat situation. Absence of a necktie would cost a 3rd Army man exactly sixty dollars. But the two GIs standing rigidly to attention were correctly dressed. The convoy swept on.

The staff car stopped and Patton strode into his HQ. Quickly his team briefed him of the events of the last few hours, as he sat on the corner of a table, toying with the handles of his twin ivory-trimmed revolvers.

Colonel Oscar Koch reported that the Germans were continuing their attack on Middleton's VIII Corps in the 1st Army sector to the north, but they also appeared to be moving into the area fronting his own XX Corps in the south.

Patton thought for a moment, stroking his

long, aristocratic nose. 'One of these is a feint,' he said. 'One is the real thing. The more I think of it, though, the more I become convinced that the thing in the north is the real McCoy.'

He looked at Colonel Maddox, his G-3. 'What do you think of it, Halley?'

The colonel was a man cast in the Patton mould. In these last few months when élite armoured divisions such as the 'Fighting Fourth' had barrelled on fifty miles ahead of the supporting infantry, he had taken the Patton dogma of, 'damn the flanks; they can look after themselves', to heart. 'It's a perfect set-up for us,' he said. 'The Germans will have to commit all their reserves to maintain this drive. That means that they can't reinforce against us or the Seventh Army. If they will roll with the punch up north, we can pinwheel the enemy before he gets very far. In a week we could expose the whole German rear and trap their main forces west of the Rhine.'

There was a pause, then Patton said, 'You're right, that would be the way to do it. But that isn't the way those gentlemen up north fight.' They knew who the 'gentlemen up north' were – Ike, Brad, Monty and the rest of the bunch whose hesitancy was preventing the Third Army from winning the war. 'They aren't made that way. That's too daring for them. My guess is that our offensive will be called off and we'll have to go up there and save their hides.'

An hour later his guess was proved right. Bradley called him personally and told him, 'Georgie, I want you to come to Luxembourg as soon as you can and bring along Koch, Maddox and Muller. I have to tell you something I'm afraid you won't like, but it can't be helped.'

The road from Nancy to Luxembourg City, the capital of the Principality, was worse than ever, crowded with vehicles hurrying north to the front, and it was late when the Patton convoy started up the *Boulevard de la Liberté*, which three months before had been called *Adolf Hitler Strasse*.

The city's appearance was transformed, the people being only too well aware that the Germans were only seven miles away. Gone were the Stars and Stripes flags, the signs in the stores announcing 'English spoken', the welcoming banners to 'Our American Liberators'.

Patton took in all the signs and noted the little groups of silent civilians at the street corners watching the convoy go by without raising their caps as they had once done. The Germans were coming back. Their leading Quislings located in Trier, thirty miles away, had been announcing it triumphantly over the German radio all morning.

The convoy passed the Hotel Alpha which housed most of Bradley's staff. Outside a long line of staff cars and jeeps stood ready gassed and packed with secret papers. GIs staggered back and forth bringing out bedrolls and personal effects. The MP guards had their fingers crooked around the triggers of their carbines.

Patton nudged Koch. 'Those guys kinda look scared to me, Oscar.'

Koch laughed drily. 'Yeah, General. But the Third Army's arrived now. They can relax.'

But Patton's appearance in the crowded war room of 12th Army Group did not seem to make any noticeable impression on the tense staff officers grouped around Bradley and his Chief-of-Intelligence, General Sibert, at the map.

There was a brief exchange of greetings and after Sibert had explained that they had already identified fourteen German divisions, seven of them armoured, Bradley broke the bad news. 'George, your Saar offensive is off. We need you up here.'

There was a tense silence. Everyone stared at the Commander of the Third Army. Now the fireworks would start. But Patton did not even protest. He shrugged, his face mirroring his disappointment. 'What the hell, Brad,' he said, 'we'll still be killing Krauts.'

Bradley heaved a sigh of relief. 'All right,

George,' he said, before Patton could change his tune, 'what can we do to help Hodges?'

Patton replied without hesitation. 'My three best divisions are the 4th Armored, the 80th and the 26th. I'll halt the 4th Armored right away and concentrate it at Longwy, beginning tonight. And I'll start the 80th on Luxembourg tomorrow morning. And I'll alert the 26th to stand by and be ready to move on a day's notice.'

Bradley nodded his approval. He had expected a bitter argument; instead he had got three divisions just for the asking. They shook hands. The conference was over.

As Mims opened the door of the staff car for Patton to get in, a young captain approached the General apologetically, 'General Patton,' he said, hesitantly.

'Yes.'

'Smith, sir. Counter-Intelligence,' he said, his boyish face turning bright red. 'General, would you kinda take it easy on the road back to Nancy. We've just got word that there are special Kraut goon squads cruising around behind our lines in American uniform.'

'So what?'

'Well, sir, we've been informed that they're out gunning for the brass.'

Patton showed his dingy teeth in a grin. He placed a hand on the young man's shoulder.

'Listen son, they're not out gunning for an old bastard like me. I'm about wound up anyway. They're out for the big brass, General Bradley, General Eisenhower. Perhaps Field Marshal Sir Bernard Montgomery himself. Who told you about these goon squads, anyway?'

'I'm afraid I can't tell you that, General.'

Patton grunted and turned to Mims. 'Okay, let's go.'

'Look after yourself, sir,' the young captain said, but no one heard him.

It was already dark when the Sherman rumbled through the ruins of the *Porte des Allemands,* the ancient gate to Metz, which bridged the River Moselle.

It had taken them six hours to cover the last twenty kilometres. Everywhere there had been Franco-American roadblocks, manned by frightened French recruits to De Gaulle's new army and bespectacled US clerks and cooks from the rearline units, hurriedly given a rifle and the job of trying to prevent German saboteurs from penetrating their lines.

Gerling remembered how his battalion had marched through that same gate in 1940. Then it had not been smashed by artillery fire and the sun had been shining. With a brass band at their head, they had goose-stepped through it – nearly a thousand men, the cream of the nation's youth, all over six foot, young, vigorous and confident, full of Greater Germany's newly won glory. Then they had come as conquerors. Now they were sneaking back under the cover of darkness as common murderers.

He dismissed the thought and concentrated on helping Hartmann get the cumbersome Sherman round the right-angle bend at the exit of the gate and through the narrow backstreets of the old town.

'Military parking over there.' It was Maier's voice over the intercom.

Hartmann saw the weakly illuminated white sign. 'Okay,' he said, 'let's park her there.'

Maier swung the Sherman round. They rumbled up the slight incline towards one of the many little squares located at the back of the great Gothic cathedral.

A slovenly French guard, an old World War One Ross rifle slung over his shoulder, a cigarette clamped to his bottom lip, ambled up to them in cast-off US uniform and muttered in broken American: 'You got permit?'

Hartman tossed him a pack of *Lucky Strikes*. 'Tout ça va,' he said.

The French soldier caught the pack neatly. 'Tout ça va,' he mumbled, his expression not changing. He strolled away satisfied.

Hartmann waited till he was out of earshot. From the Cathedral came the faint sound of the choir. 'Listen,' he whispered to the other three. 'I have to meet my V-man in the *Café de la belle Alliance*.' He consulted his notebook. 'It's just off the barracks down there – in the Rue Neuve. That's in the red light district catering for the *Caserne*, according to my information.'

'Oh, la, la,' Sailor exclaimed. *'Voulez-vous couchez avec moi, mamselle*. I pay you jig-jig.'

'Shut up,' Hartmann snapped. 'This is serious. Metz is full of agents of the Allied forces. After all,' he digressed, 'this was Reich territory till last summer and we have a lot of sympathisers here.'

Gerling did not attempt to disillusion him.

'I am to meet my man,' he went on, 'at eighteen hundred hours precisely. Now this is the plan. You,' he pointed to Gerling, 'will come with me and act as cover. When I meet the V-man, I want you watching the door. You can never trust these border folk completely. They're German when we're winning and French when the frogs are.'

He turned to Sailor. 'You take the grease gun.' The American machine pistol with the silencer could easily be hidden under his overlarge Eisenhower jacket, 'and cover the top of the Rue Neuve. Maier, you do the same at the bottom, opposite the *Caserne*. If there's trouble, I want you to make enough static to let us get away. We rendezvous here within the hour. Is that clear?'

82

'Yeah,' Sailor said lazily. 'But let's not wait too long in that street, Sarge, I haven't had a bit of tail for quite a while and I might be easily tempted.'

They split up in front of the ancient *caserne*, built by Vauban in the eighteen century and now housing a mixed company of American supply troops and the eager young volunteers from the provinces for De Gaulle's new armies. The cobbled square in front of the *caserne* was completely blacked-out. Somewhere a door opened. A shaft of yellow light fell momentarily on the pavement, and he could hear men laughing, women calling something in French and tinny *bal musette* accordion music. Then silence. Gerling gazed at the closed door in envy. If he could only be in there, drunk, careless, fumbling some whore's breast, this whole terrible mission forgotten. But he remembered the scars his body bore and the little tattoo under his arm, which would identify him for ever as one of the pariahs of the new post-war world – a member of the *Waffen SS*. For him there was no escape.

He turned into the Rue Neuve, past the green light of the prophylactic station, where a line of soldiers waited patiently to receive their treatment. Gerling knew from their lectures that if an Allied solider got VD and could not prove he had been to a 'pro' station, he was automatically given 56 days detention.

Gerling pushed his way among the drunken soldiers, boots dragging in the slush, their slung haversacks filled with the cigarettes, butter and coffee which would buy the girls who hung, heavy-breasted and hard-faced, out of every doorway.

A crowd of drunken GIs, wearing German black-leather coats with looted Lugers stuffed in their belts, held him up. They had extended across the narrow street and, swaying drunkenly from side to side, were demanding papers. One of them, a red-haired sergeant with a nasty scar running down the side of his face, kept shouting, 'You're all krauts in disguise. Who's the Brooklyn Dodgers?' He grabbed an under-sized scared French poilu by his collar and dragged him right off his feet. He thrust a hamlike fist under the recruit's ashen face. 'Who's dem bums?' he demanded aggressively.

The Frenchman twisted miserably and tried to explain that he understood no English while Gerling cast around for a way of escape. This was not the time to tangle with drunken GIs.

'*Tu viens, cheri?*'

He spun round. A whore was standing in the doorway to his left, a torch pressed below the soft bulge of her belly suggestively, the thin

84

blue light illuminating her face.

She looked like all the other whores in the street: long dyed shoulder-length hair, shaggy hip-length fur jacket, probably rabbit, and thin flowered dress, with no slip underneath. 'You wanna jig-jig, GI?' she asked with professional concupiscence, her thick-lipped mouth opened in fake passion.

'How much?' he asked.

'Five dollars American for a jump. Ten for the night. French love, I kiss, GI.'

Behind him the drunken soldiers had the French recruit on the wet cobbles and were kicking him, as he lay curled up, screaming, hands over his face. A couple of them were coming forward in the gloom looking for new victims in the crowd held up by their makeshift line. Gerling made up his mind hurriedly. 'Yeah,' he said, 'one jump.'

She came closer and squeezed his penis a little too hard. She was tired and didn't care much. 'The five dollars.' She thrust out her free hand. He gave it to her. 'Come on, let's get upstairs,' he said.

She smiled. Her teeth were bad. 'That's good. I like GIs in a passion.'

Yes, I bet you do, Gerling told himself as he followed her up the rickety stairs. They hardly get their pants over the edge of the bed before it's all over. Easy money!

She opened the door of her room. The bed was rumpled from the last visitor and there was the still smoking end of his cigarette in the ashtray on the battered dresser. She flung off her coat, kicked off her shoes and dropped on the bed which protested noisily. She opened her plump, black-stockinged legs. She was wearing no underclothes. Her eyes staring in bored routine at the ceiling, she said huskily, 'Come on honey.'

Hartmann was already waiting for him in the café. He looked up from his seat in the corner, a glass of weak French beer in front of him on the table, his eyes narrowed against the thick blue smoke. Then he looked away again.

Gerling fought his way through the mass of drunken French and American soldiers to the zinc-covered bar awash with beer. 'Un demi,' he said.

The barmaid looked at him as if he had just come out of the woodwork. 'We only speak GI here. Nix French,' she said contemptuously.

'Okay, gimme a beer,' he answered.

She leaned forward to the tap, giving him a generous glimpse of her breasts beneath the opening of her black silk dress.

Gerling grinned. Even the war had to stop for sex. He leaned against the bar, surveying the scene in the mirror behind it, savouring these few minutes out of war. He threw a glance at Hartmann. The latter appeared to be engaged with his beer, but his eyes kept stealing to the thick blackout curtain of felt which covered the door. His face was hard and set as usual. It revealed nothing.

A strange man, Gerling thought. What made him tick? He seemed to have no weaknesses, at least of the traditional soldier type – women and booze. He was as hard as his name – an ideal man for their mission. But what the hell was their mission? They were going to kill someone. An important person, Hartmann had said. But who? A civilian leader perhaps. Churchill was in London. De Gaulle perhaps?

The thick felt curtain moved. A big man, gripping an old battered leather briefcase and looking completely out of place, entered. He was dressed in a fluffy coat made out of a dyed GI blanket. Round his upper arm he wore the red and white band of the partisans. For a moment he stood at the door uncertainly.

In the corner Hartmann raised his glass of beer in toast. The 'partisan' nodded. Gerling guessed that the armband must be the identification signal. This was the local V-man.

He watched the man limp forward to shake hands with Hartmann who did not rise to greet him. The latter ordered a beer, tossing a dollar bill on the table. The two men bent their heads in whispered conversation.

Gerling watched them in the mirror,

edged with the divisional patches of the US outfits which had passed through Metz. The big man took something out of his briefcase and showed it to Hartmann, who bent over it, his high forehead creased intently. Gerling guessed it might have been a map.

The laughter and cries rose and fell like waves. A drunken GI fell to the floor and remained there, his fellow drunks stepping over him as they staggered back and forth to the *Cour,* as if he were some precious carpet on which they could not place their muddy combat boots. At the bar the blonde sweated as she filled glass after glass, not even caring whether the GIs saw her breasts or not.

Suddenly Gerling froze. There was the squeal of brakes outside; the door flew open and a white helmet came through the black-out curtain followed by an enormous MP sergeant, grease gun at the ready. 'All right, stay where you are everybody!' he ordered.

He moved in a few feet. More 'white mice', as Gerling knew the French whores called the US MPs, pushed in behind him. They were all heavily armed, as if they expected trouble.

'All right, you guys,' the big sergeant bellowed, 'knock it off now!'

'What the hell's going on?' the drunk on the floor protested thickly and tried to rise.

The MP sergeant did not even look down.

He gave the drunk a hard kick in the ribs and the man sank down again. 'Okay, let's have them ID cards and dog tags ready. If any of youse guys is on furlough here – thirty-six or seventy-two hours – I want ya leave passes too. And no crap or lip, get it.' He made a significant gesture with the butt of his grease gun.

Sullenly the GIs started to open their blouses to expose their metal dog tags and search for their identification documents. Gerling flashed a significant look at Hartmann in the mirror. His hand slipped to the shoulder 38. Hartmann's face was tense, alert and prepared like that of an animal ready to spring. His companion's was ashen with fear. This was obviously no routine check.

The policemen, clubs in their big hands, started to move among the soldiers, while the big sergeant stood at the door, grease gun at the ready.

Gerling's fingers curled round the sawn-off 38. Silently he released the safety catch, still smiling at the blonde barmaid. But his eyes were searching the café for some other means of escape. He found it quickly – the exit to the pissoir, marked *Cour*, in the corner. He gave Hartmann a slight nod and turned his head in the latrine's direction. Hartmann understood. He whispered something to his companion and Gerling could see the Frenchman's hands whiten as they gripped the briefcase. Hartmann raised three fingers slowly.

Gerling understood. Count to three – and then.

Slowly he counted three to himself and then fired. The central light shattered, raining hot splinters of glass on the crowd below. Girls screamed hysterically. *'What the hell?'* the big sergeant at the door cursed.

Gerling pushed his way through the screaming mess, kicking and punching to clear a path towards the *Cour.*

'Come on,' Hartmann yelled in German.

He felt the door fly open.

'Ce sont les boches!' a woman's voice screamed in terror.

There was a burst of machine pistol fire. Then they were outside pelting across the yard.

'There they are!' a voice shouted behind them. Lead ricocheted off the walls on both sides of the little alley and Gerling felt a hot splinter of stone sting his cheek.

'Over here,' the Frenchman yelled in Lorraine-German. 'The wall.'

Panting heavily they hauled themselves up. Behind them the noise of the MPs was getting closer. Gerling grabbed for the top. One hand just missed its ragged surface. He screamed as the brickwork tore off his nails. But he hung on desperately, until Hartmann leaned back and pulled him over. They were running down a deserted cobbled street now. In front of them, Gerling caught a glimpse of the stark shape of the cathedral between two houses. Behind them the screams of the whores and the yells of the MPs grew fainter.

'Over here!' It was Sailor, crouched in the dark doorway of a *boulangerie*. 'Quick!'

They doubled across and flung themselves into the cover, their breath coming in gasps.

'Boy, you was lucky I saw you,' Sailor said. 'You was gonna drop yourselves right in the shit. Look up there.' He pointed down the street.

Two six-wheeled US armoured cars were drawn up, their outlines faintly visible in the torches of the MPs who surrounded them.

Hartmann caught his breath. 'Where's Maier?' he panted.

'Here,' Maier's head popped out from the next doorway. He had a grenade in his hand. 'There's no use trying to get out the other end either. There's half a company of MPs there. I just made it in time.'

Suddenly a searchlight came on on one of the armoured cars. Slowly it began to probe each doorway, running from side to side of the darkened street, poking its finger in each hole, then moving on when satisfied.

'Christ,' Sailor breathed. 'What now?'

Hartmann reacted first. Standing upright,

he raised his 45 and took aim as if he was standing on some peacetime range. His aim was perfect. There was the sound of breaking glass and the light went out.

Moments later the street was transformed into a crazy battlefield, with tracer stitching the air, as the MPs fired on each other and drowned the noise of the door of the boulangerie being kicked in, and the crash of their feet as they ran through the house and out into the empty street on the other side.

Hartmann did not allow Maier to stop until the *Gruesome Twosome* had completed the long serpentine climb that led out of Metz up to the heights of Gravelotte. There, on the lonely wind-swept heights where their grandfathers had broken the power of Imperial France some seventy years before, he ordered the driver to pull into a cutting.

Maier stopped the engine and wiped the beads of sweat from his brow. In spite of the icy cold, he was bathed in sweat. He had taken his and their lives into his hands more than once in the last half hour as he had taken the ice-covered bends at speeds no tank should make under such conditions.

Now all was silence save for the howl of the wind in the trees. Down below Metz lay in darkness, not a light to be seen. The French V-man pulled himself stiffly out of the turret. In the yellow turret light, Gerling could see that he was still sick with fear. His hands were trembling.

'All right,' Hartmann said, 'I think the air's clear. You can get out now. It's a long walk...'

The Frenchman did not allow him to complete the sentence. He was only anxious to get away from these strange Germans. 'It doesn't matter,' he said.

Hartmann reached into the ammo box in which he kept their secret documents and the like – and took out a handful of French francs. He passed them over to the tall man. 'Your payment,' he said.

The Frenchman stuffed them in his pocket and, without offering to shake hands, whispered, as if the lonely plateau was filled with CIC agents, 'Good luck to you all and *Es lebe Deutschland!*'

'*Es lebe Deutschland,*' Hartmann answered.

With obvious relief the Frenchman dropped to the road and started to walk back towards Metz. He did not look back. Hartmann watched him go. Then he reached down and picked up Sailor's silenced grease gun. 'The lights!' he said.

'What?'

'Turn the headlights on, man!'

Maier did as he was told.

The Frenchman turned, peering into the thin yellow beam. Hartmann pressed the trigger of the grease gun and the Frenchman fell to the ground.

He smiled coldly at Gerling. 'Little birds sing – sing to everyone who pays them. Who knows to whom he would sing next?' He kicked Maier on the shoulder to indicate that he should start the engines again.

'But they'll find him,' Gerling stuttered.

'Of course. What of it?' Hartmann shrugged. 'The police will take him for another dirty black marketeer, shot by his pals over some deal or other. Think of those bills I gave him.'

Maier started the motors with a roar.

Hartmann clicked on the throat mike. 'All right,' he commanded. 'Let's go. We've got an appointment in Verdun.'

The Sherman rolled forward, taking the right fork after the hamlet of Gravelotte, heading for Etain.

Patton arrived home at his villa in the Rue Auxerre without mishap, but it had been a long day. He told his coloured servant, Sergeant George Meeks from Junction City, Kansas, an elderly Negro who had served him for years, to bring him a bourbon. He drank it thoughtfully and alone in his bedroom, mulling over the events of the day. He had just started to say his prayers when the telephone rang.

'Goddammit,' he cursed, his mood of humility gone. Who the hell was ringing him at this time of night? It was after eleven. But it must be important. Nobody in his right mind would risk Patton's rage if it weren't. He picked up the phone.

It was Bradley again. 'Georgie,' he said. 'Ike is coming to Eagle Main tomorrow morning for a special confab. Be there at eleven hundred hours sharp. Okay?'

'Will do,' Patton answered. He'd worry why Eisenhower was making the long journey from Paris to Bradley's forward HQ on the morrow.

He hung up and called General Gay. 'Hap,' he told his Chief-of-Staff, 'I'm going to Verdun tomorrow morning for a conference with General Eisenhower. I want you to call a special staff session for 0800 tomorrow.'

With that he said his prayers hastily and as he would tell his staff in the morning slept the night away 'like a goddam little baby. I didn't even have to get up and pee – which is pretty good for a guy of my age.'

DAY FOUR:
TUESDAY, 19 DECEMBER, 1944

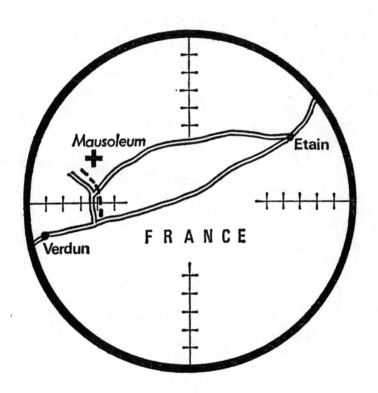

I

Although Hartmann had told them they wouldn't be coming for another hour, it was impossible to sleep on. They had all taken benzedrine and their nerves were jangling like wires. Gerling got up from his bed of branches and ferns. He shivered in the morning cold as he urinated. Hartmann, huddled in his bedroll next to Sailor and Maier, watched him but said nothing.

Gerling stamped his feet to bring them back to life and assessed their position. Five years of getting ready for battle had made this gesture habitual; it meant the difference between the survivor and the raw recruit who was killed in his first action. Quickly his eye took in the terrain.

To his left ran the dead-straight road from Etain, which they had traversed during the night, not meeting a soul. To his right, down in the fog-shrouded valley of the River Meuse, the city of Verdun. He could just make out the grey shape of the citadel poking through the mist. To their rear was the battlefield of Verdun, where in a space of ten square miles the cream of the French and German armies had bled each other white in that terrible spring of 1916.

He surveyed the road down to Verdun once more. The corner was the most likely spot. Any driver worth his salt would brake there and change down before he tackled the descent to the city, especially with the black ice gleaming on the hairpin bend as was the case this morning. He nodded to himself, making up his mind with the quick finality of the professional who had been forced to make such decisions day in, day out, for the last five years.

He walked back to the others and looked down at Hartmann. It was time to have it out with him. He wanted to know more. The knowledge might save his life. 'Hartmann,' he said deliberately, 'what exactly are we going to do?'

Hartmann looked at him with scarcely concealed contempt. 'You are an officer – an experienced officer in the *Waffen SS*,' he said slowly, as if he were explaining something to a slow and stupid child. 'You should not be interested in the why and the wherefore. All that should interest you is that we are going to ambush someone at the corner.' He pulled a hand out of the khaki sleeping bag stamped with a black 'US' and pointed to the bend. 'As I told you last night.'

'Yes,' Gerling persisted. 'I know, but I want more details. *Who* and *what* are we to ambush?'

'The *who* is no concern of yours. The *what* I can answer. It will be a small convoy heading for Verdun, made up of a staff car, probably a couple of jeeps and an armoured car in the van.'

'And?'

'Smith will take the bazooka with Maier up there,' Hartmann pointed to the height on the right of the road in the direction of Etain. 'You and I will man the Sherman.'

Gerling nodded.

'My information is that the armoured car will precede the convoy at – say – two hundred yards' distance. You and I will take it with the seventy-five. As soon as Smith and Maier hear the shot, they'll knock out the jeep at the rear of the convoy. And then,' he paused momentarily, 'we can deal with the staff car in the centre at our leisure. And let me say this. Our mission is all important for the conduct of our operations. *We cannot afford to miss!*'

II

At eleven o'clock precisely the Eisenhower convoy started through the empty streets of Verdun. The armoured car bounced up and down on the cobbles and once the MP-

packed jeep in front of him skidded danger-
ously as it rounded the bend which led to
the *Maginot Caserne,* which housed 'Eagle
Main'.

The others were already waiting as Eisenhower and his staff filed into the bitterly
cold squad room of the infantry barracks,
heated by one fat-bellied wood stove.
Shivering with cold after the warmth of the
big staff cars, they took their places opposite
Bradley and Patton, who were seated with
their respective staffs grouped behind them.

The news this morning was worse than
the day before. Sepp Dietrich's 6th SS Panzer Army in the north was battering hard at
the shoulder of the 'bulge' and below it von
Manteuffel's 5th Panzer Army was heading
for the Meuse. Already the 106th US Division had vanished, with nearly 10,000 men
ready to surrender to the Germans, and
both the 28th Infantry and the 99th were in
a bad way. Eisenhower had never faced a
crisis like this before.

He looked around the semi-circle of senior
officers, their faces as set and pale as his own.
Then he spoke: 'The present situation is to
be regarded as one of opportunity for us and
not one of disaster.' He forced a smile. 'There
will be only cheerful faces at this conference
table!'

As usual Patton was first to react. The
remark appealed to his pugnacious nature.

Exuberantly he snorted, 'Hell, let's have the guts to let the sons of bitches go all the way to Paris. Then we'll really cut 'em off and show 'em up!'

The ice was broken. Even Bradley managed a slow, leathery smile. The conference could begin.

General Strong stepped up to the map on the wall and sketched in the full extent of the German breakthrough. That finished, he handed the conference over to General Eisenhower, who explained his counter-measures to meet the German threat with equal skill and brevity. His exposé finished, Eisenhower turned to Patton. 'George, I want you to go to Luxembourg and take charge of the battle, making a strong counterattack with at least six divisions. When can you start?'

'As soon as you are through with me,' Patton answered.

Eisenhower frowned. 'What do you mean?'

Bradley and his officers shifted uneasily in their seats at Patton's ill-concealed rashness. A couple of senior British officers laughed softly at what they considered to be typical Yank showing-off. Patton would have to move 133,178 motor vehicles over 1.6 million road miles under terrible weather conditions before his army could go into action – an impossible task to the way of thinking of most of the senior officers present.

Patton seemed undaunted. 'I left my

household in Nancy in good order before I came here,' he announced.

Eisenhower nodded. 'Well, when can you start?'

'The morning of 22 December,' Patton said simply.

The effect was electrifying.

'Don't be fatuous, George!' Eisenhower snapped.

Calmly Patton puffed at his big cigar. 'This has nothing to do with being fatuous, sir,' he said slowly, letting them hang on his words. 'I've made my arrangements and my staff are working like beavers at this very moment to shape them up.'

Then he explained his plan which he had worked out with his staff at 0800 that morning. If Ike agreed, all he needed to do was to give a simple order over the telephone; his staff would take care of the rest.

'I'm positive I can make a strong attack on the 22nd, but only with three divisions, the 26th and 80th Infantry and the 4th Armored. I cannot attack with more until some days later, but I'm determined to attack on the 22nd with what I've got, because if I wait I'll lose surprise.' He pointed his cigar at the wall map and turned to Bradley who had become his pet hate in these months. 'Brad, this time the Kraut has stuck his head in a meat grinder. And this time *I've* got hold of the handle!'

With that the conference broke up. As they rose Eisenhower raised a warning finger to Patton. 'Remember, Georgie, the advance has to be methodical – sure.'

Patton showed his teeth. 'I'll be in Bastogne before Christmas,' he said.

Together they strolled out into the courtyard where the staff cars and their escorts were already waiting. Ike pointed to his fifth star.

'Funny thing, George,' he said, 'every time I get another star I get attacked.'

'Yeah,' Patton quipped, 'and every time you get attacked, I have to bail you out.'

Eisenhower gave him a wide grin but made no comment. They shook hands and parted.

Patton walked to his sedan. 'Codman, you come with me. Tell Mims we start in five minutes for Luxembourg.'

'Yes, General.' Suddenly from high above them on the bare hill, still stripped of any vegetation after the shattering bombardments of twenty-eight years before, there came the sharp crackle of small arms fire, broke by the boom of a tank cannon.

Patton stopped and listened. 'Now don't goddam tell me the Krauts have got this far!'

He turned his head to windward but the sound had gone.

Codman grinned. 'Perhaps the ghosts of the old war, General?' he suggested.

The conducting officer from Eagle Main had no sense of humour. He shook his head. 'No sir,' he said emphatically. 'That's the French Army up there, General. The recruits use it for firing practice. They've got a couple of rifle ranges beyond the old Ossuary.'

Patton started to walk on to the car. 'Surprised old Charlie allows it,' he commented.

Mims flung open the door. Patton got in. 'Okay, Mims,' he ordered, 'Lux City and make it snappy.'

'Yes, sir.'

As the car pulled away from the kerb, Patton bent his head over his maps. He had no eyes for the heights with their ominous presence from the past.

The god of war was on his side. He was going to be in Bastogne by Christmas or bust.

III

The six-wheeled Staghound breasted the height cautiously, the driver obviously worried by the steep descent beyond the bend and the thick snow flurries. A hundred yards behind it, Gerling, crouching in the freezing turret of the Sherman next to Hartmann, could just make out the olive-drab staff car a hundred yards or so behind it. Hartmann's fingers began to curl around the 75-mm's firing lever. His jaw tightened as he prepared to fire. The Staghound shuddered as the driver forced it into first gear. It came to a virtual stop as he prepared to take the hairpin bend which led to the steep descent into Verdun below, now altogether cloaked from view by the driving snow.

'Two o'clock,' Gerling said automatically.

The turret swung round smoothly with the aid of the electric driving device. The long slim gun, weighed down at the end with the muzzle-brake, halted menacingly. It was pointing directly at the Staghound.

Hartmann did not fire immediately. He had fought a lot of battles in these last five years. He had experienced the great victories of the good years and the grim defeats of the snow-covered steppes. But never had he fought a battle as strange as this, on this lonely old battlefield, where over a thousand years before the heritage of Charlemagne had been divided up by his greedy successors – a division which had meant the end of Germany's greatness for hundreds of years.

He clenched his teeth. What could be a more suitable place to fight – and win? He pulled back the firing lever. The turret shuddered. With a clatter the cartridge case tumbled to the deck. The white AP shell curved slightly upwards slowly. There was the loud echoing sound of metal striking metal. The Staghound came to a sudden halt. Thick white smoke started to pour from it. No one got out.

'You got it! You got it!' Gerling shouted excitedly, but his words were drowned by the sharp crackle of the bazooka somewhere to their rear beyond the trees. Sailor and Maier were tackling the jeep which brought up the rear of the little convoy.

Hartmann fired again. The front of the armoured car crumpled up like a banana skin. The turret flew open and a charred hand clawed its way upwards. For a moment, while Gerling watched with horrified fascination, it sought support on the glowing metal, the flames licking up all around it. Then it was gone.

Gerling recovered. 'Ten o'clock,' he snapped.

Hartmann inserted another shell and pressed the operating device. Smoothly the turret swung round to face the staff car. Gerling could just make out the driver's face in the thick snowflakes. He could imagine what was going on in his mind. Realising the trap he was in, with the jeep destroyed behind him and the Staghound burning fiercely in front of him, he swung the wheel. In the wet snow the staff car skidded sideways. At the back a door flew open. A man was trying to get out. Swiftly Gerling grabbed the 50-mm machine gun. The tracer sped over the snow and the man fell back against the door and sank to the road. The glass of the windscreen shattered and the driver disappeared behind a shining cobweb. Blinded, the driver let the big car go and it crashed into one of the oaks which lined the road. Gas started to leak from the shattered front end.

'Come on,' Hartmann cried hastily.

He grabbed Smith's grease gun with the silencer and jumped out of the turret. He dropped lightly and began running through the snow towards the scene of the ambush.

Gerling followed and in silence they ran through the snow. They passed the burning armoured car. Further up the road towards Etain, they could see the jeep, the victim of Sailor's bazooka. Smith and Maier were busy stringing out Hawkins grenades in the snow behind it to act as a minefield in case anyone was following the little convoy.

Hartmann forced open the twisted door of the staff car. The driver was slumped over the wheel, the left side of his face looking as if someone had thrown a handful of plum jam at it. He moaned. Hartmann pressed the trigger of the silenced grease gun. The driver jumped as if he had been subjected to an electric shock. He slumped back again – dead. There was not much left of the back of his head.

Hartmann flung open the rear door, kicking aside the dead soldier who slumped against it. Frantically he swept aside the smoke that poured from the car's interior. Over his shoulder Gerling could make out two men slumped in the back. There were no visible marks on their bodies. But he knew they were both dead. Perhaps his initial burst had got them.

Hartmann seized the first man. He slumped over, a thin red trickle of blood coming from the corner of his grey lips. 'It's not the general,' he cried.

He grabbed at the next man. From far away came the sudden thin wail of a siren. Up the road Sailor and Maier dropped what they were doing. Maier grabbed the bazooka and they started to run towards the staff car.

'Trouble!' Gerling cried.

Hartmann did not seem to hear. His trembling fingers were examining the other American sprawled out now in the extravagant posture of the violently done to death. 'But he's only a private!' he said flatly.

The sound of the siren was getting closer.

'For God's sake, man!' Gerling shouted. Maier and Sailor were almost up to them now.

Hartmann remained oblivious. 'It's neither of them,' he said.

Gerling stared over his shoulder at the two dead men. Both were privates and both wore the badges of the Com Z.

'There's a jeep and another one behind,' Sailor panted as he came up, the case of bazooka rockets bouncing up and down on his broad shoulders. 'We're in for trouble!'

But still Hartmann did not move. Gerling grabbed him roughly by the shoulder. 'Can't you hear,' he bellowed. 'They'll be here in a second!'

Suddenly there was a tremendous crash behind them. Gerling swung round. A thin cloud of smoke was billowing upwards.

'The first jeep has hit a Hawkins,' Sailor explained.

Gerling knew what would happen now. The other one would back off, try to find a way across the ditches and come in across country. They had only a matter of minutes to get back to the Sherman.

'Let's get the hell out of here!' Gerling roared.

'But there's no general—'

Hartmann never finished his sentence. With all his strength Gerling punched him in the jaw. His head shot back and his knees buckled under him.

Sailor sprang forward and caught him as he sank to the ground. Together he and Gerling dragged him towards the Sherman. Behind them, in the woods on the other side of the road, they could hear the jeep grinding its way in low gear towards them. But in spite of its noises and the fiery crackle

111

of the burning armoured car, Gerling could hear Hartmann's angry mumbling. He could not make out the words distinctly, but as they reached the Sherman and started to haul him up the turret, he caught one word clearly enough. It was 'traitor'.

Tenderly Hartmann felt his swollen chin and shuddered. 'My jaw hurts,' he said.

Sailor grinned and handed him a cup of coffee.

Gerling gave him a few moments. Then he said, 'No wonder it does. I slugged you.'

Hartmann took the news calmly. 'You hit me?'

Gerling stared at him. There was something about the way in which he could switch from a blinding rage to absolute calmness which bordered on madness. 'Yes, you blew your top for the second time since we've been on this mission. It's getting to be a habit with you.'

Hartmann lowered his cup and looked around curiously. 'Where are we?' he asked softly.

'Inside the great ossuary at Verdun,' Gerling answered.

'Yer, the big bone orchard,' Sailor added, as if Hartmann needed the word explaining. 'Behind there,' he pointed to the dark alcoves above which were carved the coats-of-arms of scores of French and American towns, 'there's enough bones to start up a couple of soup factories. Only trouble is they're human, including his old man's.' He jerked a dirty thumb at Maier, who had walked across the wet marble floor to the Sherman, which was parked near the great copper door that reach up into the darkness.

Maier nodded. 'My father was killed here in '16. They never found his body. He might be in there and then again, he might not. There's a hundred thousand unknowns like him behind there.'

Slowly Hartmann stared around the huge ossuary which was France's premier memorial to the dead of World War One, paid for by donations from all over the world in the twenties, when the ex-soldiers who had fought on these terrible heights had sworn there would never be another war. 'How did we get in?' he asked.

'It was Maier's idea,' Gerling explained. 'We'd soon be taken if we tried to come down from here. There are only three roads off the battlefield. The snow covered the Sherman's tracks well enough so why not try to hide out here till dark at least.'

'Yes,' Maier interrupted. 'I remember coming here as a boy soon after they built the place. My mother wanted to see where my father had died.'

Gerling nodded. 'Sailor then took over. He was kind enough to get the doors open.'

Smith held up his skeleton key in triumph. 'There you are,' he said to Hartmann. 'The divisional sign of the *Leibstandarte*. You break open yer doors with yer guns, I do it with me key.'

Hartmann didn't react. The reference to the skeleton key, a pun on the name of the first commander of the *Leibstandarte*, did not seem to annoy him, as most things that Sailor said usually did. 'Our mission has gone wrong,' he announced, his breath fogging in the icy air. 'The man I thought we were going to ambush was not in the staff car. Let me tell you a little story,' he said quietly, his hand resting on the butt of his forty-five. 'When we were thrown out of Western Europe last September by the overwhelming technical superiority of the *Amis*, the Fuehrer was not the only one who never gave up believing that we would return. There were many others – not all German – who still believed in the concept of a New Europe, united in the cause against the creeping poison of Bolshevism.'

Gerling's lips twisted in a scarcely veiled sneer of contempt. Hartmann was an intelligent man, but he had fallen hook, line and sinker for the crap spread by Goebbels and the Party's 'golden pheasants' – the brownshirted leaders – over the last year or so, once they had seen they were losing the war. He had heard this kind of rubbish in

114

officers' messes for months now. It was no longer a 'Greater Germany' but some impossible creation named a 'New Europe', which would throw back the 'Soviet hordes'. But he said nothing.

'When *Oberstuermbannfuehrer* Skorzeny's organisation pulled back under *Ami* pressure it left behind it many men and women of several nationalities – French, Belgian, Luxembourg, Dutch – who, in spite of the obvious danger, were prepared to go underground and work for us. They were mostly humble men and women, who were able to fit easily into the *Ami* organisations – a secretary here, a janitor there. Soon we had our agents everywhere, fighting their own little secret war, not for money but for the cause. Brave people who kept us informed of the movements of US commanders and their divisions, risking their lives every day for a people who had come into their countries as enemies, but whom they had learned to regard as their friends – their saviours, who had rescued them from the petty-bourgeois routine of their lives, given them a greater cause – that of New Europe – to live for.'

'*And to die for,*' Gerling told himself, thinking of the Metz V-man shot down when he was no longer needed.

'When *Oberstuermbannfuehrer* Skorzeny learned that the Fuehrer was going to strike west again, he alerted all his key men to

115

keep us informed of American military traffic, and in particular of the movements of the *Amis'* key generals – that Jew Eisenhower in Versailles, the fool Hodges in Spa, Bradley in Luxembourg and Patton in Nancy.' He made a derogatory gesture with his free hand at the mention of Patton, as if the man were beneath his contempt. But Gerling noted that he kept his hand on the butt of his big Colt. 'As a result we knew where everyone was – big or small – at six hundred hours on the morning of 16 December when our great assault started.'

'So a few hours ago, we attempted to assassinate an *Ami* general?' Sailor interrupted.

'But who?' Gerling asked.

'I know as much as you,' Hartmann replied. 'My informant in Metz had orders not to tell me.'

'Orders from whom?' Maier snapped, sudden authority in his voice.

Hartmann looked at him curiously. 'From our *Zentrale* in Luxembourg City.'

'*Zentrale?*' Gerling queried.

Hartmann smiled. 'Yes. Our whole mission has been controlled from there ever since we crossed the Sauer at Echternach three days ago! To be exact from 12th US Army Group Headquarters – *from General Bradley's own combat post.*'

IV

General Kenneth Strong got out of his car and walked up the steps to the Versailles HQ. It had been a long day in Verdun and the roads back to Paris had been hell. What he needed now was a bath and a drink. But there was to be no bath or drink for him that night. Although it was already well after eight, Betts was waiting for him in the office, surrounded by a worried group of officers.

'Problems, Tom?' he queried.

His American deputy nodded. 'Read this, Ken. We just got it in from the First.'

Strong read through the flimsy. The Germans, according to the report from his opposite number at First Army HQ, Spa, Colonel 'Monk' Dickson, were moving fast, by-passing the American islands of resistance, getting closer and closer to the gigantic US supply dumps near the Meuse which would give them enough fuel to take them to the Channel coast. Worse, Bastogne, the second road and railhead after St Vith was now completely surrounded.

He absorbed the information and passed the flimsy back to anxious General Betts. 'Is that all, Tom?'

Betts hesitated. 'I don't know whether I should bother you with it, Ken,' he said slowly. 'I don't know whether it's just one more of those goddamned rumours which have been flooding our rear areas since the sixteenth, or whether it's the real McCoy.'

Strong sat down and stared up at his deputy. 'Okay, give it to me, Tom. It's been a terrible day anyway. And it's going to be a worse night. So I might as well know now.'

'Okay, let me tell you. It's easier on the eyes. Early this morning the SS officer they picked up on the sixteenth at Liège started to sing. He stuck it out for two days until the CIC agents began to lean on him pretty heavily. He told us all, as they used to say in pulp mags.'

Strong did not know who 'they' were or what 'pulp' mags were for that matter, but he did not interrupt. He had learned long ago that Britons and Americans spoke different languages.

'He said that when he was in training at Grafenwoehr he had heard that there was a group of engineers being specifically trained to destroy US headquarters and kill the personnel there. But that was not all, Ken. He had heard a rumour, the kind of thing that always does the rounds before any new op, that there were special goon squads being trained to infiltrate our lines with specific murder assignments.'

'Did he know who the victims were supposed to be?' Strong suddenly remembered the photograph with its strange circles encompassing the four generals' heads.

'Yes?'

'Who?'

Betts looked almost embarrassed. 'I think you can guess. *Ike!*'

V

Hartmann sneaked in through the narrow gap in the huge door and stamped the snow off his boots. He wiped the flakes off his face and walked over to where they were crouched, shivering, next to *Gruesome Twosome*, trying to warm their hands over the flickering flame of the petroleum cooker on which Sailor had heated their C rations.

They looked at him expectantly. He let them wait. For a moment he warmed his hands over the flame which threw their shadows in monstrous wavering distortion on the walls. 'It looks all right outside. Black as pitch and the snow is still coming down steadily. It should muffle the noise of our engines a bit at least.'

'When are we going to take off?' Gerling asked.

'We'll give it about another half-hour, then the *Amis* will have headed to their nice warm billets. They can't stand a little bit of cold.'

'I'm not too damn good at it myself,' Sailor said.

Hartmann ignored the remark. 'Before we leave,' he said slowly, glancing from one frozen face to the other, 'there is a little bit of business I must clear up.' He grinned, an unusual thing for him. It was not a pleasant grin. He paused and then said almost conversationally. 'You see there is a traitor among us, gentlemen.'

'What!' Sailor stuttered.

'Yes.' Hartmann seemed pleased at the impact of his almost casual statement.

'Yes, you heard correctly, Smith. There is a traitor among us.' This time his voice was harder, determined. He stepped back a pace and clapped his hand on the butt of his pistol. 'Don't you think it strange that our V-man in Metz should lead us into a trap like that? If he had been a traitor, he could easily have got away in the confusion in the Rue Neuve. Of course, the police raid on the café could have been a coincidence. But what happened this morning was no coincidence. It was plain unadulterated treachery!'

Before anyone could stop him, he had stepped back and in the same instant whipped out his Colt. He pointed it at them and Gerling knew that he would use it on them, the first suspicious move they made.

While the three of them stared at him in the flickering blue light of the cooker, he continued. 'The *Amis* had set up a nice little trap for us. Fortunately we were a little bit smarter and quicker than they were. Otherwise we would be imprisoned in the Citadel now, waiting to do one last little jig on air.'

'You must be off your head,' Gerling said. 'How can you say such a thing!'

Hartmann was not offended. 'I can say it very easily. You see the *Amis* knew we would try something at Verdun, but they didn't know what. Because after our meeting with the Metz V-man, I made my own plan for the ambush and kept it secret. I'd wager that they – the *Amis* – ran a similar little convoy to the one we tackled this morning on all the roads running into Verdun. That's why we got away with our failure. The traitor had warned them in Metz what the game was. And remember that each one of you was alone in Metz for over half an hour or more before the unpleasantness in the café and could have warned the US authorities. But none of you knew which road I would take after Gravelotte – and there are at least three different ways of getting to Verdun from there.'

The softness vanished from his voice. The pistol came up threateningly. 'What do I know of you all?' he snapped. 'You, Gerling,

121

how did you spend the time between leaving the parking spot and meeting me in the café?'

Gerling had a sudden vision of black stockings and pale thighs, the sordid pleasure of that malodorous little hotel room.

'Or you, Smith? Or you? None of you are pure German. Mongrels, the lot of you. All of you have suspicious backgrounds. But one thing is sure – one of you is a traitor. Now very carefully, all of you unbuckle your sidearms and drop them to the floor. You, Smith, take that knife out of your boot too.'

'My God, you must have gone crazy,' Gerling cried.

Hartmann ignored his remark. 'I won't hesitate to shoot,' he said threateningly.

Reluctantly they obeyed his order, dropping their weapons to the floor.

'Now kick them over here. Slowly and carefully!'

When they had moved the weapons over to him to his satisfaction, Hartmann said, 'All right, you first, Gerling, unbuckle your belt and let your trousers down to the knees. And your underpants too.'

'*What?*' Gerling roared.

'You heard me,' Hartmann said calmly.

'I refuse,' Gerling hissed. 'You're off your head!'

Hartmann fired at once. The marble spurted up a foot away from Gerling. He started back, clutching his hand, blood seeping through his fingers from a cut caused by a marble splinter.

'The next time it will be your kneecap,' Hartmann said calmly, as the shot died away somewhere in the dark heights of the great mausoleum. 'Then you will never walk again.'

With his other hand, Gerling started to unbuckle the thin US belt. He pulled down his slacks and underpants and stood there, his legs slightly apart, feeling both foolish and angry. 'What now?' he snapped.

Hartman gestured with his pistol. 'Lift up the front of your shirt,' he said.

He did as he was ordered. Hartmann stared at his genitals for a moment.

'All right,' he said. 'You can pull 'em up again.'

He gestured his pistol towards Smith. 'You now.'

Without a word, Sailor pulled down his slacks and exposed his genitals.

After a moment's examination, Hartmann said: 'All right, you can button up.'

Slowly Hartmann turned to Maier, who leaned almost casually against the Sherman. 'You!' he ordered.

Gerling could see Hartmann's knuckle around the trigger. Maier could too. Reluctantly he began fiddling with the buckle of his belt. When his lower body was naked he faced Hartmann, scorn in his eyes. 'All

123

right, Major Hartmann. There you have it, you pervert.'

Hartmann was not offended. A slow smile formed on his face. 'So it was you,' he said. He waved for the other two to come closer. 'Look at him,' he commanded.

'Interesting if you like a bit of the other,' Sailor tried to joke, but Hartmann interrupted him harshly.

'Can't you see?' he snapped excitedly. 'He's our traitor! Look at him! He's circumcised.'

'So?'

'Only Jews are circumcised!' Hartmann explained triumphantly.

'Oh, God,' Gerling groaned. 'There are lots of reasons why people are circumcised – medical, social–' But the explanation died on his lips when he saw the look on Maier's face. His eyes were those of a trapped animal. Suddenly he realised that Hartmann was right. Maier was a Jew – and a traitor.

Hartmann sensed what was going through Gerling's mind. He raised his pistol level with the driver's face. Maier took his hands from his pants and raised them at Hartmann's unspoken command. The absurdity of the situation vanished. Gerling knew that this was the moment of truth. Maier had only minutes to live.

'Now my Jewish friend, you'd better start talking,' Hartmann said softly. 'Who are you? What's your game? What do your *Ami* bosses know of our mission?'

'You bastard!' Maier spat at him. 'You German bastard! One day they'll hang you.'

'That could be,' Hartmann said calmly. 'But they'll have to catch me first, your *Ami* friends, won't they? Now talk. I'll give you three. *ONE*–'

The words started to spill out. He was a Jewish newspaper man on a Berlin paper and had fled to the States in the mid-thirties. In 1941 when the States had got into the war, he had volunteered for the Army. A year later he had been sent to the OSS – the Office of Strategic Services, the US secret service – in Washington. Unlike the Harvard graduates of the capital's cocktail set, he really wanted to fight, not just talk about it. Wild Bill Donovan, head of the OSS, had shipped him to their London office in Grosvenor Square almost immediately. In the next two years he made two illicit jumps into Occupied France, helping the Maquis and the Belgian White Army. In mid-1944 he had started to train for his last mission, the present one.

'But why? How did you know?' Hartmann prompted.

Maier shrugged. 'We knew in London that in the end you would do something suicidal when you realised that you were beaten.'

Hartmann did not hesitate. He smacked Maier across the face with the muzzle of his pistol. Something cracked in the driver's nose and blood began to trickle down over his lips.

'We are not beaten, Jew,' Hartmann cried angrily. 'It is *you* who are beaten! How did you get into this operation?'

'It wasn't difficult,' Maier said thickly, trying now to stem the blood. 'I crossed the frontier below Saarbrucken. It was not tough. I made my way to Grafenwoehr like the rest of you.'

Sailor reached in his pocket and pulled out his khaki handkerchief for Maier.

'And what do you know?' he rapped.

'I know – and my people know – that you are after one of our top generals. We're fully informed. Give up, Hartmann, you've had it! Another twenty-four hours and my organisation will be on to you.' He looked at Gerling and Sailor appealingly. 'All right, he's crazy. But you guys, you're young, you're sane. You've got a chance. Why the hell sacrifice your lives for something that's been dead for months now! You–'

There was a great echoing crack. It was impossible for Hartmann to miss. Maier flew backwards, most of his face gone. While Sailor and Gerling stared at him in horror, he sank to the floor. He was dead before what was left of his head struck it.

Slowly Hartmann stuck the pistol back in its leather holster. 'I think,' he said very calmly, 'we could go now.'

Gerling stared at him. There was absolutely no emotion in his face. He stared back at the dead Jew sprawled out on the floor. Suddenly he knew, as if it had been ordained long before that one day he would kill Hartmann.

BOOK TWO: KILL!

DAY FIVE:
WEDNESDAY, 20 DECEMBER, 1944

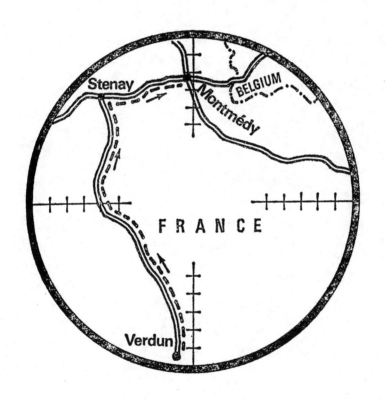

I

'The bastards – the bloody sadistic bastards!' the young CIC lieutenant swore bitterly as he stared down at Maier's body sprawled out on the marble floor. Next to the group of hard-faced MPs, the one-legged French veteran, with the ribbon of the *Medaille Militaire* in his lapel, who had found him in the Mausoleum, stood with his beret in his hands.

'It's Maier all right,' the OSS colonel said slowly. He looked at the bloody mess of what had once been the agent's face. 'That scar on his neck is listed in his personal details.'

They stepped back. The medics came forward, draped a brown army blanket over the corpse and lifted it on to the stretcher.

'Come on, Lieutenant,' the colonel said. 'Let's go outside. This place is colder than a well-digger's ass.'

In silence they strode out, their boots echoing hollowly in the great hall.

It had stopped snowing, but a low fog hung over the 15,000 graves. 'Pretty, eh,' the colonel said. He rubbed his stubbled chin. It had been twenty-four hours since he had last shaved, thirty-six since Maier's appearance in Metz had dragged him out of his bed in Spa and racing over the Belgian roads towards the French town. All for nothing. 'It wasn't so pretty when I last saw this hill in 1918. Not a tree standing in ten miles – just one great muddy hole, with bodies. Krauts and French everywhere, as far as the eye could see,' he said. The CIC man said nothing. Colonel Savage from the OSS seemed pretty long in the tooth for the cloak and dagger game.

In silence they crunched over the snow-covered gravel round the great structure which crowned the naked hilltop like some huge lighthouse. Through the porthole-like windows at knee level, the lieutenant could see the great heaps of bones – skulls, legs, arms, thrown together in hopeless confusion.

Savage caught his look. 'They say there are one hundred thousand unknown soldiers buried there,' he explained.

'Yeah,' the young man answered dourly. 'It's a long time ago, though.' The colonel understood the inference. The CIC officer wanted him to get on with it. But how did one start? How could he explain the long years which had brought him to this spot on this snowy December morning? What would the lieutenant make of a young second-lieutenant of infantry, fresh out of Harvard in 1917, eager for a scrap, enjoying every single day of the 'champagne push', as they'd called the three-month campaign in 1918 which had cost the AEF one hundred thousand casualties but which had finally got them to Sedan and the end of the war? How would he take his confession that he had been glad, unbelievably glad, when 'Wild Bill' Donovan, the head of the OSS, had rescued him from his Wall Street broker's office in 1942 and sent him to the wars again? Away from the pettiness of his private and business life with its accounts, cocktail parties and children's school fees.

He had been too old for the fighting war and, for a while in Washington, when the cocktail circuit had sneered at the OSS as 'Oh, so secret', or the 'Office of shush, shush', he had wondered if he had done the right thing. A year later in London working under the bureau chief, Colonel David Bruce, he knew that he had.

But the speeding of agents into Occupied Europe had taken its toll. The last night 'out on the town' in London, the little flask of whisky handed to the pale-faced young man at Tranmere Field, the airfield of the RAF's 'moonlight squadron', as he was strapping on his parachute. The last handshake and the old, old formula, 'We'll be hearing from you, Joe, Pierre, Heinz...'

Brave words, and how often they never came true. One by one his best agents had gone through the routine, relayed a few messages, and were never heard of again. And now Maier, the best one of all. He'd never thought the bastards would get him. How he hated the men who had done Maier to death; he swore to himself that he would get them if it were the last thing he did in this bloody war!

'Okay,' he snapped. 'Let's take stock of the situation. What do we know?'

He pulled a crumpled piece of paper out of his pocket and handed it to the CIC man.

The latter smoothed it out and read the single word on it – 'Verdun'.

'We found it about a dozen yards from the French agent they killed on the heights of Gravelotte. That's our only clue to their direction. That other thing,' he jerked a thumb towards the site of the ambush, 'tells us they were in a half-track or a tank.'

'Yeah. It could be either. There are plenty of White half-tracks mounting 75-mm cannon these days.'

'And naturally whatever vehicle it was, it bore US markings. Did your people find any trace of them after they left here last night?'

'Negative.' The lieutenant shook his head. 'Not with that snow. It covered all tracks up here. And down on the road. Hell, they're driving bumper to bumper down there. They'd cover all tracks.'

Colonel Savage absorbed the information. 'Okay, where do we go from there?'

'Well, it's pretty obvious, Colonel, that they were after one of the big boys at the Verdun conference yesterday. Eisenhower, Bradley or perhaps Patton.'

Savage nodded. 'Of course, but which one? Or all of them? Eisenhower is being taken care of. He's back at Versailles and his counter-intelligence boys are going to keep him there for the next couple of days until we've sorted out this darned "Operation Grab" thing. So that leaves us Bradley and Patton, and they're the most likely targets. The direction of our defence has passed out of Ike's hands now. It's in those of the generals who are going to carry out the counter-offensive against the Krauts.'

'That makes sense.'

'So in our area of operations, we've got Bradley and "Blood and Guts". They're the men the Krauts would dearly love to eliminate, especially now, after yesterday's decisions.'

Colonel Savage looked around carefully. A group of medics stood around the box-like ambulance which was waiting to carry away Maier's body. But no one was close enough to hear them. 'I can't tell you everything, Lieutenant. But yesterday one major decision was taken at *Maginot Caserne*. Patton and Bradley are to kick off a push to relieve Bastogne. It's planned for the 22nd. And I guess you know just how important for the whole battle the relief of Bastogne is?'

'Yes sir,' the CIC man said smartly. 'AFN said this morning in the news that the 101st are completely surrounded there. Once the Krauts take them they control the roads to the Meuse. And after that there's nothing to stop them till they hit the coast.'

'Right. But I don't want the big boys wrapped up under tight security at this moment in time. Bradley and especially Patton should have the freedom of movement they require. We can't have them burdened with a couple of battalions of MPs hanging around them. So I'd like you to get on to this first and try and locate the Krauts before they get anywhere near Patton's or Bradley's HQs.'

'No deal, sir,' the lieutenant answered. 'I've already been on to 9th Air Force. They're socked in. And the fog's gonna get worse in the next two days. They don't expect any break in it till about the twenty-fourth. So it's no use asking them – even for Piper Cub spotter planes.'

Colonel Savage was silent for a moment as he absorbed the information. Down below the medics were opening the back of the ambulance. The one-legged French veteran was moving stiffly down the snow-covered steps of the great mausoleum. 'All right, Lieutenant, you take Patton's HQ at Nancy. Check out the situation there. I'll go to

Bradley's HQ at Luxembourg. I can liaise with your Captain Smith there.'

'He's a good man, Colonel.'

'But one thing, Lieutenant. The Krauts have got a man there. Who I don't know! Perhaps a clerk, a driver, a janitor. But one of those civvies is the guy who is passing the info about the movements of the big boys. How else could the Krauts have known about the Verdun meeting?'

II

'I've never seen anything like it,' the WAC captain said in her thick throaty voice, which indicated too many cigarettes and too much booze. 'I was stopped three times not more than the two hundred yards from my apartment. The first guy stopped me on the Boulevard de la Liberté and asked me who was Betty Grable's latest husband.' She coughed and lit another cigarette with thick ugly fingers. 'How the hell should I know! I'm not interested in him.'

Yeah, the pale-faced sergeant clerk thought to himself as he listened to Captain Bertha Vinnenberg's diatribe, you're not interested in him but it would be different with Betty Grable! He looked at the heavy-set stenographer who was General Bradley's private secretary. She was a butch if ever he had seen one.

'And just as I was passing the Hotel Alpha, some little kike stopped me for the third time and asked me what state I came from. When I said Maryland, he asked me what the capital was. I said Baltimore and he passed me on – the stupid little Jewish bastard.'

The sergeant clerk sighed wearily. Captain Vinnenberg would shoot her mouth off about the Jews at the drop of a hat and he was in no mood to listen to that crap this morning. He had had a bad night. His girlfriend, Anna-Marie, had given him the air; she was scared the Germans were coming back and she didn't want to have anything more to do with the 'American liberators' of the previous September. So he had hit the booze and now he had a lousy head. And if that weren't bad enough, General Bradley had given him a hard time because he had forgotten to fill up the coal-bucket which supplied the stove in his office.

'The old man's in a helluva temper this morning,' he said, interrupting the woman's flow of words.

Captain Vinnenberg forgot her pet hate. Behind her thick glasses her eyes lit up with interest. 'Why?' she asked eagerly.

The sergeant noted once again how Vinnenberg was always interested in what the general did. She was one of those secretaries who submerged herself completely in her boss's work because she had no other interests outside of her job.

'He got bad news yesterday, I guess.' He laughed, then winced as the pain threatened to burst his head. 'Mind you, Captain, he doesn't take me into his full confidence, but I guess from what I hear around here that Montgomery has got the First. That leaves him with Patton's Third.'

'Oh, the poor dear,' she said, a look of real if comic concern on her big face. 'That means Montgomery has more American troops under his command than General Bradley.' She clicked her tongue furiously like some old schoolmarm. 'It's not right that General Eisenhower should do that to General Bradley after all he has done for him.'

'Tell it to the Chaplain,' the sergeant told himself cynically. But he did not utter the sentiment aloud. WAC Captain Bertha Vinnenberg could be a bitch if she wanted to and she had powerful friends at 12th Army HQ. More than once he suspected that she had been instrumental in getting a couple of the clerks who had made cracks about her gross masculine appearance behind her back transferred to line units. With the word out that the brass was combing COMZ rearline personnel for riflemen for combat outfits, he knew when to keep his mouth shut. He did not fancy a transfer up that one-way road at this particular moment. Yesterday's confidential figures had shown that the average replacement only survived three weeks at the front – and he wanted to live a little longer yet.

'Yeah,' he said, 'it's hard on the old man. But you know how those guys at SHAEF are. Eisenhower is the British best general after all!'

Captain Vinnenberg nodded grimly and pulled at her uniform blouse, which was too tight for her and rode up to reveal her large bottom when she leaned forward. 'Can I go through now?'

He nodded. 'Yeah, the General's expecting you.'

As she passed the large wall mirror just outside General Bradley's office-door, she took a quick glance at herself. Satisfied with what she saw, she gripped her pad and pencil and knocked.

Behind her back the sergeant grinned. 'What a piece of ass,' he thought. 'Wonder if she's ever had it.' He shook his head in mock sadness. 'No, nobody would want to get in those drawers.'

'Come in,' Bradley called.

Smartly she stepped inside and said, 'Good morning, sir.'

'Morning,' Bradley said grimly.

Obviously the 12th Army Group commander was angry. His usual friendly smile and polite greeting, which had endeared him to his staff from GI upwards, were absent. Hardly looking up at her, he pushed a sheaf of papers – handwritten notes, full of erasures and corrections – towards her. 'For my private diary,' he snapped. 'Get them typed up and give me a fair copy by twelve hundred hours.'

'Yes, sir,' she said.

'I'll look at them straightaway and let you know if I'm satisfied with them. As soon as you get my okay, destroy the originals. And don't take any copies, understand.'

'That's not routine, sir,' she protested.

'I know it's not routine,' Bradley snapped. 'Nothing is routine today, Captain.' He caught himself. 'Excuse me, but it's been a trying night and morning,' he apologised.

'I understand, General,' she said soothingly.

'I've just had a call from Smith, the CIC man,' he explained. 'Apparently there's a bunch of Nazi killers out to get me.' He smiled bitterly. 'A good time to do so, the way things are at this present moment. And according to Smith they're getting word on my movements from some civvie spy working at my HQ. Hell, there's a good couple of thousand of them working here. It could be any one of them.'

'Just over fifteen hundred to be exact, sir,' she corrected him with her maddening concern for accuracy.

'Hm. Well at all events Smith would like us to be specially careful with our documents – things like the war diary and the like.'

'Will do, sir,' she said efficiently. 'Anything else, sir?'

'Yes, General Patton will be coming here tonight for dinner. He's motoring up from Thionville where he spent the night. I want you to see that he gets a good steak dinner.'

She made a quick shorthand note on her pad.

'And what about Bourbon? Are we well fixed for it?'

'Yes, sir. I think you've got a couple of bottles of the good stuff left in your private stock.'

'Fine.' Bradley sighed and ran his hands through his thinning hair, as he recalled the shock of the pre-dawn conversation with Ike's Chief-of-Staff, Bedell Smith, which had resulted in his First Army being taken away from him and given to that damned little Britisher Montgomery, with his holier-than-thou attitude which had plagued him for these last six months. 'Well, I guess that's all.'

'General,' Captain Vinnenburg said with unusual hesitancy for her.

'Yes?' Bradley looked at her severely.

'It's the Christmas Party, sir, for the Lux kids. All the girls and guys in the office have decided to give two bars of *Baby Ruth*, one stick of *Life Savers* and a *Oh Henry*–'

She never finished the list.

'*For God's sake*, Captain Vinnenberg!' Bradley exploded. 'Here I am trying to control the destinies of a quarter of a million men in the middle of a surprise German counter-attack and you worry me with some goddam civvy Christmas Party!'

'I'm sorry, sir. I'm sorry,' she stuttered. But there was a strange light of triumph in her eyes.

III

All day they had zig-zagged back and forth along the third-class country roads of Northern France heading for the border with Luxembourg. Over and over again they had spotted Allied roadblocks just in time and had backed off swiftly in the thick ground fog. Twice angry shots had followed them, but they had ricochetted harmlessly off their armour plating. Yet in spite of the fact that the countryside north of Etain seemed to be full of second-line enemy soldiers, they gradually drew closer to the hills which Gerling knew indicated the start of the French Ardennes and the border with Belgium and Luxembourg.

They clattered on down narrow but dead straight French country roads, taking to the fields every now and again when they felt that there might be an enemy roadblock ahead. But in spite of the close calls which kept Gerling sweating with fear, there was a tense silence among the three men. Sailor was driving now, but his usual Hamburg talkativeness was gone. He replied to Hartmann's orders with monosyllabic, non-committal grunts.

Gerling knew why. The seaman had got on well with Maier. They were both NCOs, a natural team against the two SS officers. Now he was alone, and although he recognised the necessity of killing Maier, the brutality of Hartmann's method had shocked him.

Hartmann did not seem to notice Smith's silence. Once more he was the cool, efficient tank commander, speaking only when necessary, keeping his orders to the minimum, hardly raising his voice even when they had blundered into a French checkpoint in the fog. Sailor had thrown the big Wright Whirlwind engine into reverse and shot the *Gruesome Twosome* down the road as if the devil himself were after him. Gerling, tense and sweating, caught a glimpse of Hartmann's face. It was completely expressionless.

Just after four, as the fog was beginning to clear, they started to approach the heights ahead and Hartmann ordered Sailor to cut the engines. They had just skirted the town of Stenay. Sailor got out of the leather driving seat and came up stiffly to where Gerling and Hartmann stood surveying the stark outline of the hills. 'We're about a dozen kilometres from the border – a kind of three-country border. Over to the left there – that's Belgium. And over there,' Hartmann pointed to the north-east. 'That's Luxembourg. It's a tough border to guard. There are dense woods on both sides, as you can see.'

Gerling nodded, but didn't say anything. Sailor remained silent too. He sensed that Gerling now shared his own hatred of the cold-blooded SS major. Both of them now knew Hartmann for what he was – a ruthless pathological killer.

'Before the war,' Hartmann continued, 'it was a smuggler's paradise. If we were on foot, it would be easy for us to cross the border into Luxembourg. We could simply walk through the forest. But we're not.' He paused and pointed to the stark outline of the firs marching across the hills like disciplined rows of infantry. 'There's a road up there I remember from 1940. A country road with no villages or anything along it, save for an old Vauban frontier fortress. If the French are guarding the road, they'll be stationed there. They are a predictable people, you know.'

If he expected a comment he was disappointed. Neither of his listeners spoke.

'Perhaps I'm being too cautious. If there are French up there, they might be asleep by the time we try to pass. Perhaps they have already run away. They know our troops are coming soon.'

For once Gerling agreed with Hartmann. From the north there was the faint rumble of guns at the front and as he peered at the horizon, it was lit up regularly by faint pink flashes.

'But we must find out,' Hartmann went on. 'The tank would give us away at night. We'll get as close as possible and then go the rest of the way on foot to check the place out.'

Sailor spoke for the first time. 'And then what?'

'If there are not too many of them, we shall deal with them.'

'Without me!' Sailor snapped. 'I've had enough killing – I have had a noseful.'

Hartmann took his reaction calmly. 'There are other ways of dealing with anyone we might find there,' he said.

'How do you mean?'

Hartmann bent down to the box which contained their money. He fumbled in it for a second and pulled out what looked like an American thermite grenade. 'A new type of knock-out gas,' he said, 'developed in *Obersturmbannfuehrer* Skorzeny's laboratories at Friedenthal. Assuming that we find the fort occupied, we wait until the French are all in some confined space – say a barrack room or a canteen – and then toss this in. According to our scientists, they'd be out to the world in sixty seconds. They'd sleep for the next three hours and wake up with nothing more disastrous than a headache.'

Sailor took the grenade. 'Let's have a look at it,' he demanded.

Hartmann smiled at him, but there was no warmth in his eyes. 'No bloodshed at all, my friend. I can assure you of that.'

They crept carefully up the narrow winding path, paved with ancient cobbles dating back to the seventeenth century when the hilltop fortress had been built. On both sides were crumbling stone houses, shutters clamped down over their windows, as if they had been long abandoned. Yet they knew that that was not so.

'You can smell the garlic through the goddamned walls,' Sailor whispered, his old humour returned since Hartmann had given him the gas grenade. 'God knows how those frogs can stand it!'

As they approached the silent outline of

149

the fort which crowned the height Gerling felt glad that Sailor was at his side. There was something threatening, foreboding about the stillness of the place.

They almost walked into the sentry. He was asleep in a small stone pillbox built into the side of the gate wall, a tiny charcoal brazier at his feet. Hartmann put out his arm and stopped them just in time.

In the glow of the brazier, they could see he was a young man. Perhaps some seventeen-year-old recently called up by General de Gaulle in his desperate attempt to reform *la Grande Armée* and play some role at the side of his two major allies.

Hartmann nudged Sailor. 'All right, Smith, he's yours. You can try your new pacifist approach on him,' he whispered cynically, 'as long as he doesn't make any noise and warn the rest.' He jerked his thumb at the dark passage which led into the fort. As he did so, Gerling caught a glimpse of his eyes in the light from the brazier and he realised that Hartmann had fooled them.

Cautiously Sailor stole forward, his Colt gripped in his big fist. His knife, the easiest way of settling a sentry without noise, was still stuck in the top of his combat boot.

Suddenly Gerling saw the sentry begin to stir. In the ruddy glare of the brazier he could see the man's eyelashes flicker. Slowly he opened his eyes. For what seemed ages, he stared at the crouched figure of the German in sheer disbelief, as if this thing could not be happening to him. With all his strength Sailor hit him in the stomach. The breath left him in one great gasp and he doubled up. As he went down, his helmet rolled off and Sailor caught it neatly with his free hand before it fell to the cobbles. In the same instant he brought the butt of his Colt down on the youngster's skull. There was a dull grunt and the boy's knees buckled under him. Gerling dashed forward and caught him just before he hit the ground. Gently he lowered him the rest of the way.

Sailor bent down to look at him. He straightened up and spat on his bruised knuckles. 'He'll live to fight again,' he said.

'How neat, gentlemen,' Hartmann said cynically. 'You should have both been in the Medical Corps.'

They ignored his remark, passed on through the low gate and entered the fortress itself. In reality it was a little street of tall seventeenth-century houses grouped around the church-cum-citadel in the typical Vauban manner. Most of them, the three men saw immediately, were empty, their walls pocked with shell-holes from the battles of the previous summer like the symptoms of some strange skin disease. But at the end of the cobbled street, a battered American truck with French Army signs was parked under the light emerging from a tall unshuttered window from which came the sound of several voices.

'So, the Frogs are here in full force after all,' Sailor said.

'Yes,' Hartmann agreed. 'And their security is lousy – like most things French. They've probably never heard of the blackout.'

Gerling started working his way in the shadows towards the yellow light, stopping at every window and door and casting a quick glance inside. The other houses seemed empty. Hartmann, following him, whispered, 'They've probably only got a platoon here. I doubt if many people use this frontier save the locals.'

'Yes,' Gerling said, 'it looks like that. But let's see what we're up against before we make any decisions. I'd rather tackle another way across than get involved in a shooting match against superior forces.'

Moments later they were crouched around the window. Hartmann nodded to Gerling and tightened the grip on his grease gun. 'I'll cover you. Check it out!'

Cautiously Gerling raised his head and peered through the dirty window. About a dozen French soldiers sat round a long wooden table in the centre of the room, grouped round the flickering yellow light given out by an ancient brass paraffin lamp. Four of them were playing cards with the all-consuming interest of soldiers the world over, while the rest, pipes and cheap cigarettes stuck in the corners of their mouths, watched. On the bunks behind them a couple of men snored, their mouths wide open. He searched the room for their weapons and saw them lined up in a wooden rack in the shadows at the rear. They were secured by a metal rod driven through the rack and secured at each end by a padlock, the key of which was probably in the pocket of the fat sergeant who was grinning with triumph as he slapped down a winning card.

Gerling slipped down again. 'A dozen or so,' he whispered urgently to the other two. 'Most of them grouped round the table. All of them appear to be without weapons.'

'Good,' Hartmann said. Swiftly he started to rap out his orders. 'All right, this is the plan. Smith, you throw the grenade. Try to get it under the table.'

'How? Through the window?'

'No, that would dissipate the gas. That would be no good. We'll do it through the door. I'll cover you with the machine pistol.' he turned to Gerling. 'You keep your eye on them through the window. If they try to make a move, use your pistol. But only if it's necessary, naturally. We are trying to make this operation as humane as possible, aren't we?'

Gerling did not bother to reply. He prepared to cover them.

'One other thing,' Hartmann said. 'If when Smith has thrown the grenade you can smell a kind of fruity odour, for God's sake hold your breath! That's the gas, and I don't want to wait for three hours until one of you wakes up.'

The other two nodded.

Sailor and Hartmann ran to the wooden door. Gerling leaned his shoulder against the wall and peeped into the barrack room. They were still playing cards. Out of the corner of his eye he could see the wooden door. Suddenly it flew open. He caught a quick glimpse of Sailor's arm. The next moment the grenade flew in. It fell to the floor just in front of the table. There was a slight crack and it fell apart. A thick stream of gas started to emerge from it.

The men at the table scattered in alarm. All was confusion and noise. A chair fell. Another man blundered into a bed. The sergeant fumbled in his pocket, probably for the keys to the rifle rack. But not for long. A moment later he grabbed at his throat. His eyes bulged from his face. Horrible gurgling sounds came from his throat as the thick gas rose higher. They were paralleled by those all around him as the other French soldiers breathed in the gas.

His face pressed against the window, Gerling watched with horrified fascination as the first man fell over the table scattering the cards. Another followed him, little flecks of foam splattering everywhere as he dropped clutching at his throat. Then the sergeant slumped down. Gerling could see the blood seeping through his lips. Obviously he had bitten his own tongue through in his agony.

One by one the young French recruits were overcome, their faces hideously distorted, their loose denims suddenly black and damp at the front where they had involuntarily urinated, their arms and legs jerky and unco-ordinated as they tried to stagger in vain to the door.

Gerling caught a slight whiff of the gas through the broken pane. He started back immediately as the fruity smell Hartmann had spoken about assailed his nostrils. Almost immediately his pupils contracted and a filmy haze hampered his vision. 'For God's sake,' he cried aloud, staggering towards the others like a blind man. 'That wasn't a knock-out gas... It's burning my eyes.'

Hartmann caught him by the arm. 'Pull yourself together, man!' he bellowed, now his old self again, the fake humility gone. 'Of course it wasn't. It was *Tabun!*'

Even in his agony, the terrible realisation of what they had done flashed through Gerling's mind. He remembered the lecturer's description of *Tabun* during his officer-cadet days in Bad Toelz. 'It is a nerve gas, a pale brownish liquid, which destroys the enzyme cholinesterase. Thus the message-carrying function of the nerve is destroyed. The first symptom is a staggering gait, followed by vomiting and involuntary evacuation of the bowels. Death can follow within a matter of minutes.' The men who a moment ago had been swimming in gas like fish in a hazy aquarium were already dead, murdered in the most hideous way known to man!

'You bastard, Hartmann!' Holding himself up against the wall and vomiting wretchedly, Gerling heard Sailor spit out the words bitterly. *'You lying murderous bastard!'*

Gerling forced himself to look up, the vomit dripping from his open mouth.

Sailor had drawn his pistol. It was pointing directly at the pit of Hartmann's stomach. The latter's face was ashen pale. There was no escape now. Gerling shook his head to rid himself of the nausea. He could see Sailor's finger crook around the trigger of the Colt.

'You're a swine,' Sailor said calmly. 'I knew that when you killed Maier.'

Gerling knew he should try to stop Sailor. But he knew too, that he no longer cared. Men like Hartmann were not worth saving. He deserved to die.

'I'm going to count three,' Sailor said, 'and

then I'm going to shoot you, you rotten bastard!'

'But you can't. I'm an officer. We're German. Our mission, think of our mission!'

But Sailor was not to be stopped. 'One,' he said firmly and tightened his grip on the pistol.

'No,' Hartmann screamed and raised his hands in front of his face.

'Two!'

Sailor was about to fire. Gerling saw his jaw tighten as he raised the pistol.

Suddenly a shot rang out and Sailor's body jerked. 'Thr–' the word died on his lips. Slowly the pistol began to slip from his fingers.

Hartmann reacted first. He whipped the grease gun from his shoulder. In one movement he turned and fired. The sentry they had knocked out at the gate was thrown bodily against the wall from whence he had fired. The rifle clattered to the floor. He clutched his stomach with a soft moan and fell to the ground.

In that same moment Sailor fell too. Gerling sprang forward, his eyes still hazed with tears from the nerve gas. Sailor lay sprawled on the cobbles, his breath coming in short shallow gasps. Gerling tore at his clothes. There was a huge hole in his chest. Sailor was dying, he knew, but all the same he fumbled for his field dressing.

Gently Sailor clutched him by the wrist. 'It's no use, Captain,' he whispered weakly. 'I'm a goner.'

In the yellow light from the window, Gerling could see the sailor's nose turn white at the end. Smith had a matter of moments to live.

'If you ever get to Altona, let my folks know...' His jaw fell down. The eyes went blank and rolled upwards. Gently Gerling lowered his head to the wet cobbles. He was dead.

Hartmann looked down at the dead man and then at Gerling. For a moment he said nothing. Thus the two men, the kneeling officer and the dead sailor appeared as if frozen in some melodramatic tableau in a cheap provincial theatre. 'We must go now,' Hartmann broke the silence.

Gerling pressed down the dead sailor's eyelids. He could not see Hartmann's machine pistol, but he could sense the silencer a matter of inches from the back of his head. He knew too that Hartmann would not hesitate to use it on him. He took one last look at Smith.

'Good-bye, Sailor,' he said softly.

'Come on,' Hartmann said.

Together they turned and hurried down the little cobbled road. They came to the gate and stepped over the dead body of the sentry who had killed Smith. As they turned the corner Gerling told himself that the man at his side had only hours to live.

Four hours later they rolled into Luxembourg City. Hartmann directed Gerling as if he had lived in the city all his life. Confidently he ordered him through a mass of twisting backstreets and alleys until they came to a stop in a cobbled courtyard not far from the great ravine which runs through the capital.

'All right,' he snapped through the intercom. 'You can switch off the engine. We're here.'

'Here?'

'Yes. This is the *Zentrale*.'

A few moments later Hartmann was ringing the bell of a medium-sized eighteenth-century house. It was a long time before anyone answered but finally Gerling heard the sound of heavy footsteps coming down a long corridor towards the door. A chain was removed and a bolt pulled back. It opened to reveal a bright white light which blinded Gerling for a moment.

'Who's that?' a voice asked in German, clear German not the Luxembourg form. The voice belonged to a woman. Gerling blinked his eyes.

'Vinnenberg?' Hartmann queried.

'Yes.'

Hartmann clicked his heels in the German

fashion. 'May I introduce myself – my name is Hartmann.'

There was a sudden warmth in the woman's voice. *Hartmann,* I have been waiting for you a long time. Come in quickly.'

Hartmann moved forward. Gerling finally managed to focus his eyes, strained by the gas and long drive through the blacked-out country roads to Luxembourg City. A big bespectacled woman of about thirty-five was standing at the door. She was dressed in the uniform of a captain in the United States Women's Auxiliary Corps!

DAY SIX:
THURSDAY, 21 DECEMBER, 1944

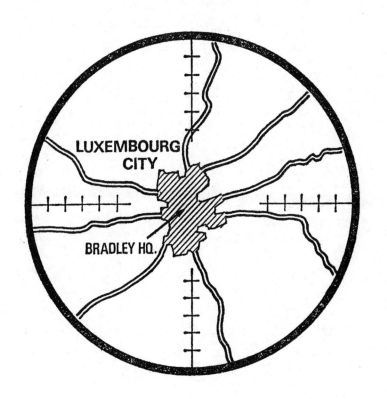

I

The four of them sat round a big black table in the centre of a stuffy overfurnished living room, a low-hanging lamp casting its light on their faces and leaving the rest of the place in darkness.

Gerling was exhausted, yet the strangeness of the scene kept him awake.

The WAC captain he now knew was the mysterious *Zentrale*. Her 'companion', a pretty, simpering Luxembourg girl called Simone, giggled every time they spoke to her.

'Don't worry about her,' the WAC captain said, 'she's a fool, but a pretty one, eh?' She looked proudly at her 'companion' and laid her heavy hand on the girl's naked arm. 'She can't speak a word of English. But she's loyal. If she has one bit of political interest in her brain, it'd be for us,' she added. 'Her father volunteered for the *Waffen SS* as soon as we liberated Luxembourg in forty. He's been missing in Russia since forty-two. Hasn't he, you poor darling.' She patted the girl's arm again. 'But now you've got me to look after you.'

Again the girl simpered and showed her pretty white teeth but she said nothing.

163

'Get rid of her!' Hartmann snapped, scarcely able to conceal his disgust at the relationship.

'*Geh mal, Schatzi,* the WAC Captain said softly, her German perfect save for a slight, hardly noticeable American accent.

Obediently the girl rose and left the room, swinging her hips provocatively as she went. In spite of his exhaustion Gerling felt a slight sexual stirring, but he knew that there was nothing for him in that direction.

The American woman waited till she had closed the door behind her. Then the smile vanished from her face. 'Listen,' she said aggressively, staring directly at Hartmann. 'Get this into your wooden head, once and for all. I'm the boss here!' She poked a dirty forefinger at her massive lumpy bosom. 'I'm doing the planning!' Again the finger against the bosom for emphasis. 'And I'm sticking my neck out so that you guys can pull off the operation! *Understood?*'

Hartmann lowered his eyes. 'Yes, I understand,' he said softly, but Gerling could almost physically feel his rage. 'Can we get down to business now.'

Slightly appeased, the captain took a piece of paper from inside her uniform blouse and handed it to Hartmann. 'That's your man,' she explained.

Hartmann stared at the little slip of paper. 'So *that's* the one!'

'Yes. He is the one who could put an end to our operation in the Ardennes if he is not eliminated soon.'

She gave Hartmann another moment to study the paper, then she reached across the table and took it from him. She rose and, crumpling the paper into a ball, flung it into the stove in the corner. 'All right, come over here.'

Like two obedient schoolboys they crossed the room to a wall on which hung a large scale map of the front. 'That's Bastogne. Over there – that's St Vith. Both are within fifty miles of here.'

As she sketched in the details of the situation in the two key towns, Gerling had to fight hard not to laugh. She sounded and acted just like some crusty old general with the purple stripe of the general staff down the sides of his pants, save for one thing – she wore a skirt.

'Thus,' she was saying, 'with both towns surrounded by our troops we can expect them to fall soon. My information at HQ is that St Vith will last a matter of hours. But Bastogne is a little different. There the Americans are beginning to react – slowly admittedly, but they are reacting.'

'How do you mean?' Gerling asked.

'Yesterday they decided at Verdun to turn the troops Patton has on the Saar front loose. They'll be used to relieve Bastogne.'

Hartmann groaned. 'If that swine Maier hadn't...'

'That's history,' the WAC captain snapped, interrupting him. 'Here are the details. Eisenhower has ordered three divisions, all belonging to the US III Corps, to lead the counterattack. In particular, the armour will cause our commanders trouble. It's the Fourth Armored Division. It's the best the Army's got.'

'When do they kick off?' Hartmann asked.

'On the morning of the twenty-second.'

'So we've got thirty-six hours to stop him.'

'Yes.'

'Have you any suggestions?' he asked. 'Where is he now?'

'Somewhere in town.'

Hartmann's eyes lit up. 'Let me have details.'

Gerling looked at his watch through blurred eyes. It was nearly two in the morning. He felt as if he could sleep for years. 'If it's all right,' he said groggily, 'I'm going to turn in. I can hardly keep my eyes open.'

The woman looked at him contemptuously. Her thick lips twisted in a sneer. 'Another male weakling eh,' she said.

Hartmann did not look away from the map. 'All right, Gerling, you can go,' he snapped, his voice as fresh as if he had just slept for eight hours. 'I can manage this without you.'

Wearily Gerling dragged himself to the

couch in the other room which the woman had assigned to him. With the last of his strength he pulled off his combat boots and then stretched out, still fully clothed, on the big sofa. Moments later he was deep in a heavy sleep.

When he awoke in the morning, Hartmann was gone.

II

'We've got one of the bastards!' The young CIC captain crashed through the door of the office Bradley had assigned to Savage in his Luxembourg HQ without knocking.

Savage put down his paper cup of coffee – his breakfast – and stared up at Smith. 'What did you say?'

'The French reported finding him an hour ago in an old fort near Montmedy on the border between...'

Savage waved aside the explanations. 'Yes, I know the place. But who and where is he?'

'He's dead,' Smith said sorrowfully, 'and a dozen French soldiers with him. Gassed!'

Savage stared at the younger man incredulously. 'Gassed?'

'Yeah, that's why I guess it's one of them. The doc has just made a preliminary examination of the corpses of the French soldiers, but his guess is that they were killed by a nerve gas – Sarin or Tabun. They're both on the Kraut secret list – and we haven't got them. So the conclusion is obvious – the dead guy in US uniform that was found at the scene of the massacre must have been one of their agents.'

'Yes, of course,' Savage said. 'So now we know where we stand. They – or what's left of them – are on their way here. Perhaps they're here already. They've already shown how efficient and brutal they are. I want every man you've got put on to this. We're going to throw a screen around 12th Army Group HQ at, say, five hundred yards' distance. Everyone, US or civvies, who enters that area is to be searched.'

'That's a tall order, Colonel. I don't know if we...'

But his sentence was cut short by the hard metallic chatter of 20-mm cannon fire. Almost in the same instant the high-pitched Continental air-raid sirens started. Savage dashed to the window. Aluminium foil was fluttering down from the sky like a cloud of sparkling exotic butterflies, meant to fool the American radar. But it wasn't the foil which caught his eye. It was the four radial-engined Focke-Wulfs weaving in, line abreast, at five hundred feet!

Down below the anti-aircraft gunners

scampered madly for their half-tracks, mounting the banks of half-inch machine guns. But they were too late. Violent lights flashed along the wings of the enemy planes. Savage ducked and the windows of his office shuddered. Fragments of glass showered down on him. 'I've been hit,' Smith yelled above the roar of the planes.

Savage swung round. Smith was holding his shoulder and blood was seeping through his fingers. Savage rushed over to help him but he stopped half way and dropped to the floor. Another group of Focke-Wulfs were coming in, zooming directly at the HQ at four hundred miles an hour. A line of machine-gun fire stitched a pattern on the opposite wall. Plaster and blunted lead flew everywhere. Down below in the courtyard the HQ guard had reached its half track. A sergeant jumped on the seat and the multiple machine guns went into action. The noise of the guns and the snarl of the fighter-bomber engines was terrific.

The Germans came in time and again, their cannon crackling viciously as they dived, zoomed up and tore round in their desperate attempts to knock out the vital HQ. Savage dragged Smith against the wall, then crept back to the shattered window.

The sky was full of the planes' white contrails and the brown puffs of anti-aircraft fire. Below the gunners were sweating over their guns, swinging them frantically from left to right, as the Germans came in first from one side and then from another.

Suddenly the gunners struck lucky. A Focke-Wulf had lowered its wheels and lifted its nose. Savage recognised the drill. In this way, the pilot could keep the speed of the plane down for a fraction of a second while he did some deflection shooting. It was only a brave and experienced pilot who would tackle such a manoeuvre. For this one moment his underside marked by the black iron crosses, would be in full view of the gunners.

The sergeant manning the gun below, recognised his opportunity. Suddenly, with a blinding roar, the fighter-bomber exploded. One moment it was there. The next it was gone. A strange shape catapulted past the window. It was the pilot. A split second later he crashed into the wall of the house opposite at over six hundred miles an hour. A great red stain spread over the white stucco wall. Then the raid was over.

'Hell, we've never had an air-raid here since I arrived in Lux,' the wounded CIC man said. He looked at the doctor probing his shoulder to discover whether there was any metal left in it. 'We called Lux the last air-raid shelter in Europe. The last people to bomb this place were the US 8th Air Force just before we moved in.'

Savage said nothing. He absorbed the information thoughtfully and watched the doctor tend to the boy's arm. Behind him Bradley's sergeant clerk wielded a broom inexpertly, trying to clean up the mess. He was not making a very good job of it.

The phone rang and Savage seized it eagerly. It was the call he had been waiting for for the last five minutes. 'Savage,' he said and listened attentively.

His face relaxed and he breathed a sigh of relief. 'Thank you for the information,' he said and replaced the receiver.

Smith looked at him expectantly but Savage shook his head and with his eyes indicated the bespectacled doctor, now busy placing a field dressing around the young man's upper arm. He patted it professionally. 'Well, I guess that'll get you the purple heart, Captain,' he said, and handed him a bottle of tablets. 'Take one of these every three hours. They'll kill the pain. If you have any trouble, come and see me.'

Savage ushered him to the door. 'All right,' he turned to the clerk. 'Would you leave us. I'll need you in a moment though, so don't go away.'

The clerk shouldered his broom and followed the doctor.

Savage turned to Smith. 'I just got word that General Bradley is okay and General

Patton had just left for a conference with his corps commanders before the air-raid started.'

'Thank God for that.'

'But, God knows what we're going to do about Patton. He's off to the front in an open jeep with no escort whatsoever. He and Mims, his driver, are running the war all by themselves, it seems.' He shrugged in defeat. 'But we'll let that one take care of itself. We've got a more important problem on our hands.'

Smith frowned questioningly.

'It's pretty obvious, isn't it?' Savage said. 'That air-raid was deliberately staged to put either Bradley or Patton, or both of them out of action before the Bastogne operation started.'

Smith looked at him round-eyed. 'You think so?'

'I don't *think* so, Smith. I *know* so!' He pulled a tattered flight map out of his pocket. 'While you were being attended to, the gunners outside found this in what was left of the Focke-Wulf.' He threw it on the table and Smith picked it up and stared at it. It was the sort of thing fighter pilots used for navigating when they were going cross country. He turned it fold by fold, tracing the pilot's route from an emergency landing strip on the other side of the Trier at the little Moselle town of Wittlich, across the border near Echternach and directly following the big motor-road from there to the capital. The last section was an accurate sketch of the centre of the capital, the bridges obviously being used as guides for the pilot. The Hotel Alpha and the railroad yard HQ were ringed in red. Savage, who had followed his progress, nodded. 'Yes, just what you think. The only two places they attacked were the Alpha and here. It might have been a coincidence, but I don't think so. Our friends who killed Maier are in the capital and they have contacted their key agent here.' He thumped his fist down on the table with unusual emphasis for him *'Here!'* he said once more.

Smith said nothing. He waited for the colonel to continue.

'We know this place is full of illegal transmitters,' Savage went on. 'It wouldn't have been too difficult for our killers to contact Wittlich Field and get the raid laid on for this morning when they knew the two big guys were here. Wittlich's only ten minutes flying time away. It was a planned aerial assassination – a regular hatchet job from the air! So, do you think you are well enough to help me?'

'Of course, sir,' Smith replied. He could already see his performance report with the statement, *underlined,* 'In spite of his wound, Captain Smith insisted on remaining at his post and contributed materially to the success of our mission. Captain Smith is recommended for the next grade...' He dismissed the thought and concentrated on the task at hand. 'What can I do?'

'Well, this is the way I see it. There were only a limited number of people here last night who knew that General Patton was to stay the night. You know as well as I do that the move of his Third Corps up to Belgium is still classified.'

Smith nodded.

'And that the order is to keep him undercover as much as possible. With Patton, mind you, that's like trying to hide the Statue of Liberty.'

Smith laughed dutifully.

'But as far as General Bradley's HQ goes, only a handful of HQ personnel knew he was to spend the night here. Most of them had gone back to their billets by the time Patton arrived last night. Okay, let's have a look at those who might have been in the know! Let's get that sergeant clerk in first. But before we do, what do we know of him?'

Smith grinned. 'Professor of Librarianship at some mid-western university before he was drafted. Hobbies – books naturally – and girls. Back home he's much married – five kids.'

'Any record?'

Smith shook his head. 'No, not really. He

got gontac in London in '43 and had it privately treated by a limey doctor. Against regs naturally. But that's all.'

'Okay, let's have him in.'

The ex-Professor of Librarianship entered with the broom in his hand. 'Do you want me to finish the job, sir?' he asked, indicating the floor.

'No, you can put down your broom.'

'Yes sir.'

'All right, Sergeant. You knew that General Patton was going to spend the night here, didn't you?'

'Naturally, sir. General Bradley gave me the job of fixing up his accommodation. He got the General Eisenhower suite on the second floor of the Alpha.'

'Okay, who else knew that General Patton would be staying here?'

The ex-Professor looked at Savage curiously. But he concentrated on the question. 'Well sir,' he began ticking them off with his fingers. 'There were the two cooks who were on night shift. The clerk in charge of quarters. Naturally the staff who attended the dinner.'

Savage nodded to Smith. 'Get me their names,' he ordered.

Smith left the room.

'Who else?'

'Well Mims, the general's driver, the mess waiters and, of course, Captain Vinnenberg.'

'Who?'

'General Bradley's private secretary. She's a WAC captain, sir.'

'All right, Sergeant.' Savage said, 'let's see you get on the stick and earn yourself a seventy-two hour pass to Paris. Get them all in here within the next thirty minutes.'

'*Paris?*' the sergeant's face lit up.

'Sure thing. Pig alley and all – if the Krauts don't get there before you,' he added *sotto voce*.

But the ex-Professor did not hear. He rushed to the door, repeating the magic word to himself, 'Paris.'

III

As the jeep, mud-encrusted like the tanks of the 4th Armored it was passing, its only distinguishing mark the three silver stars of a lieutenant-general, dodged yet another Sherman, Sergeant Mims turned to Patton and said, 'General, the government is wasting a lot of money hiring a whole general staff. You and me has run the Third Army all day and done a better job than they do.'

Patton, huddled in his tan raincoat in the open jeep, his head narrowly missing the 50-inch machine gun mounted behind him every time he moved to take another salute from 4th Armored officers, grunted. 'Yes, you might be right there, Mims. But we still can't change the weather. That goddam chaplain obviously didn't have an in with God after all.'

Mims grinned as he swung past a clattering half-track filled with armoured infantry, their faces pinched and red with cold. Willy Meeks, Patton's servant, had told him the story how the boss had summoned Chaplain O'Neill to him and told him that he was sick and tired of his soldiers having to fight the weather as well as the Germans. 'See if you can't get God to work on our side.'

The Chaplain had protested that it was 'going to take a pretty thick rug for that kind of praying'.

'I don't care if it takes the flying carpet,' the Old Man had snorted. 'I want you to get up a prayer for good weather!'

Brigadier Holmes Dager, one of Patton's favourite commanders, whose Combat Command B of the Fourth had done fine work in the dash across France, was waiting for Patton when he got out of his jeep. Dager swung Patton a fine salute and waited to hear why the Old Man had taken it into his head to pick on him for a visit.

Patton did not mince words. 'All right, Dager,' he said, 'I've picked you to lead the fourth into Bastogne.'

Dager said nothing. He did not dare to object that most of his Shermans were falling apart from the long months in combat and that his armoured infantry was full of replacements, some of whom had never even seen a tank before they had been posted to him.

'Give me your map,' Patton said.

He stared at the confused scrawl of red, blue and black chinagraph arrows on the cellophane map cover for a moment, then jabbed a gloved forefinger at a spot just south of Bastogne. 'There are two roads into Bastogne,' he explained. 'The Bastogne–Neufchâteau one and the one to Arlon. I'm going to send the Fourth up the Arlon one. The idea is that the French will clear it and relieve the 101st.'

Dager knew that breaking through was not the major problem; the major problem would be how to keep the road free once the heavy armour had passed into Bastogne. The road was self-sealing, once the Germans came creeping back to be faced only by the following supply vehicles. But again he did not object; it was not wise with Patton in his present confident hell-for-leather mood. He had already heard what Patton had said at the corps commander's new HQ yesterday. He had turned to the assembled officers and snarled: 'Everyone in this Army must understand that we are not fighting this battle in any half-cocked manner. It's either root-hog or die. Shoot the works. If those Hun bastards can do it that way, then so can we. If those sons of bitches want war in the raw, then that's the way we'll give it to them!'

Dager contented himself with asking, 'What role is the CCB going to play in this, General?'

'You will move up the secondary roads west of the main highway parallel with the CCA, along the ridge lines. If 'A' gets held up, you take over, understand?'

'Yes sir,' Dager shouted, as another convoy of armoured infantry started to roll by.

Quickly, Patton began to sketch in the details of how he wanted the attack mounted, while Dager made rapid notes on his clip-board pad. When he was finished Dager put away his pencil. 'When is H hour, sir?' he asked.

'We attack with Third Corps at six.'

Dager felt a thrill of excitement at the words. He raised his hand in salute as Patton strode back to the waiting jeep. Mims was already revving the engine.

Just before it left, Patton leaned round and said, 'By the way, Dager. I'll be at the line of departure to see you off.'

Dager's protest at the danger of that meeting was drowned by the noise of the jeep taking off. Seconds later it had disappeared into the mass of vehicles rumbling towards the sound of the guns and the battle of the morrow. Shaking his head at such foolishness on the part of the Old Man, he walked back to where his officers were waiting. 'All right,' he said solemnly, 'we kick off tomorrow morning at zero six hundred. And if that isn't enough, gentlemen, old Blood and Guts himself is going to do us the honour of speeding us on your way.'

'His guts – *our blood*,' a junior staff officer muttered, but Dager pretended not to overhear the remark. He bent over the maps. 'All right, shall we get down to it?'

IV

The sergeant clerk brought Savage his fifth cup of coffee that morning. It seemed as if he hadn't stopped talking for the last three hours. Every five minutes the sergeant clerk had ushered in another one of the HQ's staff who had known that Patton had spent the night at the Hotel Alpha. Cooks, clerks, servants, secretaries – he had checked them all out with Smith's aid. But so far he had turned up nothing very much save that the movements of the US Army's top commanders were known to a hell of a lot of

180

people – so many that he wondered how any classified information was ever kept secret.

'How many more have we got, sergeant?'

'Six, sir. Four military – Pfc Lissak and Corporal Jones of the MP battalion in charge of guarding the Alpha, the desk clerk, Higgins, Captain Vinnenberg and the two Lux civvies responsible for cleaning the area. They were on a GI party – I mean cleaning up last night,' he corrected himself quickly, 'when General Patton arrived last night. They saw him for sure.'

'Okay, I'll see the military personnel last. Let's have the civvies in first.'

The sergeant closed the door behind him and faced the remaining six, seated on the hard wooden GI trestles. He pointed at the first of the civilians, an old man dressed in cast-off fatigues. *'Okay, du, Hermann, Gehen du rein,'* he ordered.

Obediently the old sweeper rose and shuffled towards the door.

The sergeant clerk grinned at Captain Vinnenberg, proud of his German and happy with the knowledge that he would soon be off to Paris. 'Only way to treat Krauts. Give 'em a clear-cut order that they understand.'

Captain Vinnenberg sighed. 'How many more times have I to tell you, Sergeant, that they're not Krauts. Luxembourg has been a completely independent state for over eighty years now. It just happens that they speak a German dialect that's all.'

Mentally the sergeant told the WAC what to do with her information. Aloud he said. 'I'm sorry, Captain, I keep forgetting.'

Vinnenberg nodded seriously, as if she were accepting an apology for a personal front. 'What's going on in there anyway?' she said conversationally. 'The Old Man'll be blowing his top. I've been out of the office over an hour now.'

'No sweat, ma'am,' the sergeant said easily. 'Colonel Savage has cleared that with General Bradley.'

'Sergeant, I asked you a question. What's going on in there?'

The sergeant hesitated. He glanced at the closed door. Then he moved closer; it didn't do to offend the bitch. She was an important person at HQ. 'Something to do with the air-raid this morning and the people who knew that General Patton stayed here last night.'

Fortunately the door opened that moment to allow the elderly civilian cleaner to leave. The sergeant turned to his companion. *'Du jetzt,'* he ordered and missed the look of alarm which momentarily crossed Captain Vinnenberg's face.

She gave it two minutes. Almost casually she rose and put her shoulder bag under her arm. 'I'll be back in a second,' she said.

The sergeant looked at her. 'Captain,' he said hesitantly. 'I got orders not to let anyone leave.'

'It's only for a second, Sergeant,' she said softly. To put him at his ease, she took a *Camel* out and lit it slowly, breathing out a stream of blue smoke, as if she had all the time in the world. 'I'm going to the little girls' room.'

'Where?'

'The little girls' room – the latrine,' she added, a little more firmly.

'Why?' he asked stupidly.

'To take a piss!' she retorted. 'How stupid can you get?'

The two MPs sitting opposite her looked at her, shocked. The sergeant flushed crimson. 'Then I'll have … have to come with you.'

'Sure,' she said easily, 'you can hold my goddam hand if you want. All I know is that I can't hold my water any longer. Come on!'

She swept out, followed by the sergeant. Behind them the MP corporal chuckled. 'Boy, ain't she just something!' he said to his companion.

Captain Vinnenberg sat firmly on the seat of the lavatory, puffing furiously at her cigarette, her mind racing. The OSS colonel had obviously discovered the morning's air-raid was not just a coincidence, but a planned murder attempt. He had found out too that the only way the raid could have come about was with the connivance of someone within the HQ. What if they had access to her prewar record? What if they discovered that her father had been born in Germany and had only come to the States when she was ten? Could they also find out that she had joined the *Bund*, the German-American Nazi organisation after she had returned to Chicago from the Olympic Games in Berlin in '36. For a moment she thought of that glorious summer which had changed her whole life. It had been in Berlin that she had first discovered she was different from other women. She didn't want a man always pawing her, fathering children, reducing her to the level of a sow in a farmyard. In Heidi's arms, that wonderful blonde *Führerin* with her cunning, exciting fingers, she had learned what love really was about. Suddenly she had been happy, really happy, for the very first time in her whole life. She forgot the snide jokes at her dumpy figure and short hair the clerks in the office were always making behind her back; her foolish housewife of a mother's continual worried questions about when she was going to get married. A lot of things had started to fall into place. Her father's death in that black August of '29 when he had shot himself after the Jews had started wanting the money back they had loaned him for his shoe factory. Heidi had explained that one; how the Jews had deliberately murdered her father in order to take over his business. It was typical of them. The kikes were everywhere, perverting, corrupting, distorting, in their efforts to assume world power.

Heidi had taught her, too, that she need not be afraid of being different. In the ranks of the woman's organisation 'Beauty and Belief', in which she was a leader, there were many like they were – women who wanted their own lives, independent of male whims and dirty sexual desires – who could go their own way without the male crutch.

That summer, set against the awe-inspiring world of Berlin, had changed her whole personality and purpose in life. One year later when the *Abwehr* had asked her to work for them, she had jumped at the chance. In 1941 when the Jew Roosevelt had dragged America into the war, she had followed their instructions immediately and joined the Army, leaving her well-paid secretarial job without the slightest regret. The rest, until she had been planted in 12th Army HQ in England in early '44, had been easy. The little German kike refugees who filled the ranks of US counter-intelligence had been too busy making out in their nice safe billet behind the lines to dare to worry her, secretary to General Bradley himself.

But now the inevitable had caught up with her. If only she could get out of the HQ and reach Simone she would be safe. Simone could smuggle her out of Lux. Within an hour they could be with the advancing Germans who were only a few miles away now. Through the small barred window of the latrine, she could hear the rumble of the German guns.

'Captain,' it was the sergeant, his voice tinged with embarrassment, 'are you gonna be much longer in there?'

She glanced round the dark cubicle. The window was too small and was barred anyway. There was no way out there. Suddenly she thought of the scissors. She opened her khaki slingbag and pulled them out. The General was always concerned about his personal publicity. Ever since he had passed the 1st Army Group to Hodges and taken over control of the whole Army Group, he had kept a keen eye on the write-ups in the papers and it was one of her daily duties to check through the military newspaper *Stars & Stripes* and cut out anything about him. Hence the scissors.

'Coming, Sergeant,' she said.

She took her powder compact in her left hand and held the scissors behind her bag in the right.

'I was just making myself beautiful for the interrogation,' she said and patted her face as if she had just made it up.

The sergeant muttered an embarrassed, 'Didn't mean to rush you, Captain. But Colonel Savage is interviewing the fellows from the provost company now.'

'I see.' She moved towards him in the dark corridor which led to the latrines as if to accompany him back to the waiting room.

The sergeant fell into step with her. They had only gone a few yards when he heard the clatter of something metallic falling to the floor. He stopped and saw that the captain had dropped her compact on the floor.

'Oh excuse me, I'm so careless,' Captain Vinnenberg said apologetically, fumbling with her bag. 'I wonder if you would…'

'Sure,' he said easily and bent down to pick it up.

Vinnenberg glanced up the corridor. No one in sight. No sound, save for the routine clatter of the typewriters in the main typing pool. She raised the scissors. Her mouth open wide, as if she were gasping for air, she brought them down. The resistance as they passed through the cloth of his blouse was hardly noticeable. He gave a grunt. Blood spurted up round the scissors and the man's knees buckled under him. As she pulled them out blood shot up and stained her blouse. With a barely audible groan the man hit the floor.

Then she was running, her skirts hitched up high, as she had never run before, the slingbag dropping from her shoulders unnoticed as she headed for the door.

V

Savage rose stiffly from the dead clerk's body. 'Okay, it's the woman Vinnenberg then!'

Smith shook his head in amazement. 'Jesus, would you believe it? A woman – an American woman betraying us to the Krauts.'

Savage ignored the remark. He walked past the dead sergeant, took the bag from the clerk who had found the body and opened it. It concealed the usual things – lipstick, comb, ID card, special headquarters pass, peppermint drops – and something less usual – a wad of badly developed and amateurishly posed photographs, all of the same two people. One was a gross woman in her mid-thirties whose dark horn-rimmed spectacles contrasted grotesquely with her naked body; the other was a much younger woman, blonde and pretty in a plump way.

Colonel Savage flicked through them swiftly then turned to an MP corporal. 'Go and find me the senior WAC officer – and tell her it's urgent!'

The WAC major was grey-haired and gentle. She shuddered as she saw the body.

'My name's Savage,' the colonel introduced himself. 'Sorry to drag you in on this, but I need your help.'

'Certainly,' she said in a weak voice.

'Captain Vinnenberg.' He held the photos out.

'Oh my God!'

'Is it her?'

She nodded. 'Yes. But you must understand that there are always a few lemons in any outfit. That kind of person is inevitably attracted...'

'Okay. So she was a lesbian,' he interrupted, knowing that time was running out. 'Where can I find her? Captain Smith of the CIC reports she's not in her billet. We've got a couple of patrols out looking for her in the city. But it'd be a help if you could tell us if she had some place to go to.' He indicated the photographs. 'To the place of the girl here, for example.'

The major pulled herself together. 'I knew she had a friend, a civvie girl. But I don't know where she lives. One thing might help though. That photo there.' She pointed to a ludicrous shot of Vinnenberg in uniform with the girl in a flowered dress perched on her lap like some absurd parody of the typical domestic scene of the 'little woman' and 'hubby' just home from the office, 'It was taken in Lux City.'

'How do you know?'

'That tower, or whatever you'd call it, in

the background. To the left of their heads. Well, it's part of the Grand Ducal Palace.'

'Can you pinpoint it?'

The major's brow wrinkled. She held up her hands, then twisted them, as if she were trying to work out the direction.

'Okay,' he cut her short. 'We'll find it. Thanks for the help, Major. Just one thing though. Would Captain Vinnenberg have known the details of General Patton's movements today and tomorrow?'

'Oh yes, as far as the situation allows a fixed plan at the moment, she would cerainly know. Captain Vinnenberg was a very efficient secretary. She knew everything.'

VI

Hartmann's face was twisted with rage. Ignoring Gerling and the girl he bellowed at Vinnenberg, his whole body shaking with anger. 'You fool – you damned fool,' he roared at her. 'Why the hell did you come back here?'

'I had to look after Anne-Marie. I couldn't leave her here.' She put her hand on the girl's arm protectively. Anne-Marie looked back and forth between Vinnenberg and Hartmann in bewilderment.

'Don't you see that they'll follow you here?'

'They don't know about this place. It belongs to Anne-Marie's parents. They think I live in the WAC billet.'

'You damn fool!' he yelled.

'Live in the WAC billet! Do you think they don't know you're queer. They know all about you and that silly cow.'

'Don't you dare talk to me like that, you pig!' Vinnenberg yelled back. 'What the hell do you know about love?' She turned to the girl. 'Get a bag packed, Anne-Marie. We've got to get out of here before the police come.'

Anne-Marie hurried obediently out of the room and Gerling could hear her running up the rickety stairs to the bedroom.

Hartmann grabbed the WAC's shoulder and spun her round. 'Where is he now?' he demanded.

'At the front,' she cried angrily, thrusting off his hand. 'And don't put your filthy paws on me.'

'Where?'

'How the hell do I know.' She walked over to the drawer of a writing desk and started to pull papers out of it.

'What do you know about his movements?'

'Nothing for today. He's everywhere and nowhere.' She pulled out the wad of dollars she had been looking for. 'All I know is that he's going to be there when the Fourth kicks off its attack tomorrow morning.'

'Where?'

'I don't know,' she shouted. 'For God's sake, leave me alone. I'm finished with the whole damned operation now. It's all yours.'

Beside himself with rage, Hartmann grabbed her by the shoulder. 'Don't think you can back out of the operation now, you ... you pervert! Now think – *where?*'

Suddenly she was icily calm. 'Did you say pervert?' she said slowly.

She turned to Gerling, seeming to notice him for the first time. 'When I was given this mission by the Reich Security Main Office, I demanded to know everything about the man who was going to lead it. It was important to know every last thing about his mentality.' She smiled icily. 'I found it out well enough – and more.'

She turned back to Hartmann. 'I know all about you,' she said. 'And you have the nerve to call me a pervert. What about the business with the whore in Lille? Or that little episode in Minsk with the Russian girl? How old was she when they found her body? Fifteen?' She laughed mockingly. 'All of fifteen years old! Of course she was a third class citizen. So it didn't matter. They sent you to the front again. But in forty-three in Berlin after you received your Knight's Cross... That saved your head, you know.' Her mouth twisted in a cynical smile. 'And you dare to call *me* a pervert!'

Suddenly she was aware of the demented look on Hartmann's face and sensed her danger. She opened her mouth to scream but his back-handed blow across her neck killed it at its source.

'Bitch, perverted bitch!' Hartmann roared. He swung his fist hard. Her false teeth flew from her mouth and her glasses shattered. She sank to the floor, blood pouring from her nose.

'My God,' Gerling yelled. 'Have you gone mad?'

Hartmann swung round, raising his arm to protect himself and Gerling's fist struck him harmlessly on the shoulder. For several moments they grappled, Gerling straining every sinew to get his hands to Hartmann's throat. Hartmann twisted desperately but he could not escape Gerling's hands. Hartmann's eyes bulged. His mouth fought desperately for air. But Gerling did not relax the pressure. Hartmann, he knew, was dying, and he wanted him to die. That was all he could think about – Hartmann dead.

In one last desperate effort, Hartmann brought up his knee. It crashed into Gerling's groin. He flew back, the pain running through his body like fire. He doubled up, his hands clutching his crotch. The next instant Hartmann's foot crashed into the side of his face and everything went black.

He came round to the sound of a police siren and loud hammering at the door. He shook his head and stared at the shambles of the room. 'Open up,' a voice was saying a long way away. 'Open up this door!'

He staggered to his feet. His crotch still hurt like hell. He walked a few steps. Then he stopped. At the end of the room lay Captain Vinnenberg, dead. Her clothes had been ripped off her. Her legs were open wide and a thick rod, probably used to pull the blackout curtains, had been thrust between them.

Gerling stared down at the mutilated body in numb incomprehension.

'If you don't open that door, I'll blow the lock off!' a voice shouted from below. Then as if to someone else, 'All right, Sergeant, shoot it in!'

A shot rang out from below.

'All right, you've done it,' the voice said. 'Now give it a heave with your shoulders.'

Gerling looked round for a way out. Downstairs was obviously no good. He grabbed his Colt and hurried to the door where the sound of booted feet greeted him from below. Deprived of any choice, he ran upstairs, his panic somehow killing the pain in his groin.

The door to the girl's bedroom was open.

She lay sprawled on the bed, most of her face gone, her flowered dress soaked in blood. Hartmann had let her have a full burst with the silenced grease gun. The empty cartridge cases littered the floor.

He flung open the window. Outside was the typical Luxembourg iron-railed balcony. It was thick with dirty snow, as if it had not been used for months. He looked up. There were fire hooks protruding from the steep slate-covered roof. The tilers used them to fix their ladders to on repair jobs. He swung himself up on the railing. Down below there was a drop of twenty metres. Gingerly balancing on the tips of his toes, he reached up.

Inside the house the noise of the searchers was coming closer. He heard them pause when they found the captain's body. Then heavy boots began climbing the stairs to the girl's bedroom. Desperately his fingers grasped the hook. His arm trembling under the strain, he heaved himself up, kicking the shutter to with his right foot. As he pressed himself against the tiles he heard the door burst open in the room below him followed by a gasp of horror from his pursuers at the sight of the girl's body.

Slowly he started to draw himself up the steep roof, twice sliding back down the slippery tiles almost to the gutter. In the end he reached the chimney, gasping for breath, his nails torn and bleeding. But he knew he could not wait. They would be out searching the garden soon. He bit his lip as he measured the distance between him and the next house. It was too risky. There was only a matter of a metre between the two houses but he knew that he would never be able to hold himself on the other roof.

Crawling along the top of the roof, he stopped at the edge and peered over. There was a deep chasm between the two houses.

He remembered his training at the SS Cadet School in Bad Toelz. The business with the SS honour-dagger had been bad enough in the first week – fifty press-ups with an upturned dagger held, point upwards, under the new cadet's chest. Then had come the grenade test, exploding a stick grenade on the top of the cadet's helmet. If one did not tremble, kept perfectly upright, the grenade splinters would fly harmlessly to all sides. If, however, the cadet wavered, there was one more vacancy at the mountain academy. That had been followed by the tank test. Each cadet had been ordered to dig a foxhole – 'a damn deep foxhole', the instructor had bellowed with an unholy grin on his face – within ten minutes. Precisely ten minutes later a squad of old-fashioned Mark II tanks had rumbled up and begun to turn and twist over the holes. It had been just too bad for the odd cadet who had not managed to dig his hole deep enough. Gerling had managed to overcome all the tests. But the climb down the sheer rock chimney in the Bavarian Alps above Garmisch had nearly broken his nerve for good. The sick agony of that nightmarish climb up the slippery rock had haunted him for many a night afterwards.

He stared down the dark abyss. Below he could hear the cries of the MPs as they spread out into the garden, looking for a Hartmann who was long gone. Taking a deep breath, he stuck his legs out into space and gingerly began to feel for a hold with his feet. Slowly he began to lower himself until his shoulders were wedged against the stone.

Time and time again waves of panic and nausea flooded up and threatened to overcome him. But he kept on, fighting the wall and the tremendous strain on his back and legs. Little by little he crept downwards. Bit by bit the evil-smelling corridor at the bottom of the abyss came closer.

Suddenly a voice below said, 'Do you think he might have gotten over the wall?'

Out of sight, somewhere beyond the division between the two houses, another voice answered, 'Hell, no man, where ye got ya brains – up ya ass?' There was the sound of someone spitting contemptuously. 'How could he? The bastard's still somewhere in the house, believe you me.'

There was the sound of a match being

scratched across a stone surface. Crouched between the two walls, his muscles threatening to burst, Gerling caught a glimpse of a sputtering pool of light as the match fizzled and went out. There was a cough and someone breathed out gratefully.

'Okay, let's get on the stick,' the voice said, 'You take the front of the garden. I'll check the back.'

'Roger, Sarge.'

The boots crunched over the hard snow.

Gerling continued his crablike process down the wall. He was only two metres from the ground when his shoulder muscles gave way completely and he fell in a heap into the snow-covered midden between the two houses.

Moments later he was shinning over the furthest wall of the other house. He ran silently to the spot where they had parked the tank behind a great pile of wood. The *Gruesome Twosome* was gone.

DAY SEVEN:
FRIDAY, 22 DECEMBER, 1944

I

The terrified sentry panted along the cobbled road. Behind him, between the trees, the permanent barrage flickered a soft pink. An American machine gun on the outskirts of Bastogne chattered with monotonous patience.

The sentry ran awkwardly in his thick overcoat and clumsy overshoes, his sidearm clattering against the brass of his belt. His breath coming in short frightened gasps, he turned into the shattered Belgian farmyard which housed the armoured infantry command post.

The door of the barn refused to open. 'Christ Almighty!' he cursed in his panic. The rattle of the SP was getting closer. He tugged again at the jammed door. Inside the exhausted GIs who had spent the last thirty-six hours in open trucks slept on unheeding. His fingers were frozen and he couldn't get them into the crack of the door. In despair he swung his boot against it and blundered in as it flew open. The SP must have reached the edge of the village now. The men sprawled fully dressed in the straw stirred uneasily.

He spotted the CO lying in the middle of

the room, a dirty brown blanket drawn up over his head.

'Sir,' the sentry panted. 'Captain Haig, wake up, sir!'

The officer did not move. In the corner someone said, 'For Jesus' sake, knock it off!' Roughly he grabbed the officer's shoulder. 'Sir, please sir, there's...'

His words were drowned by a terrifying roar that ripped the night apart. A soldier shot bolt upright, his eyes pressed firmly together. The barn trembled. Then the blast hit it. What was left of the glass in the blanket-covered windows shattered, showering the sleeping men. As the CO emerged from under his blanket, the sentry yelled at him, 'There's a Kraut SP in the village, sir.'

The German self-propelled gun attached to the 5th Parachute Division which was holding the road to Bastogne in front of the 4th Armored's startline buried itself in one of the snow-covered ruins, its gun pointed directly at the hopeless confusion of vehicles which jammed the little square ready for the attack.

It opened fire, systematically blocking any attempt to get out of the square by blasting the outer vehicles. Men ran out of the surrounding houses and barns, struggling with their equipment. Within seconds all was confusion, noise, flames, death. In vain men tried to start their vehicles. The motors were too cold. Others dashed back to the safety of the cellars, filled with scared civilians. NCOs bellowed conflicting orders. An officer, clad only in shirt and pants, seized a bazooka and attacked the Ferdinand. The rocket bounced harmlessly off its 'bazooka pants', as the GIs called the German extra armour. Next moment his chest was ripped apart by a burst of machine-gun fire.

In a doorway, three soldiers under the command of the company's top kick watched another GI running for his truck cut down by the German machine gun. The burst was followed by the crack and roar of the cannon and the truck disappeared in a burst of yellow and red flame. The men in the doorway ducked hastily. Fragments of metal and stone pattered down on their helmet liners.

The top kick had had enough. 'All right, you guys. See that cannon.' He pointed at a slim-barrelled anti-tank gun standing abandoned some one hundred yards from the German self-propelled vehicle. 'We're gonna get that Kraut bastard with it.'

'I've never handled an anti-tank gun before,' one of the men said. 'I was a cook till last week.'

'Well, you'd better learn goddam quick,' the top kick yelled. 'Come on!' The four soldiers raced for the cannon. The top kick grabbed hold of the little anti-tank gun's trails. With a jerk he undid the lock and pulled them apart.

'Come on, jump to it!' he grunted.

Two of the men took hold of the trails and let them drop. With a metallic clang, the spade-ends hit the cobbles and dug themselves in. The top kick flung himself behind the shield. Three shells were attached to it. He freed a shell, jerked down the breech-lever and shoved the cartridge home. 'Jesus, I hope these bastards are armour piercing!' he muttered to himself as he clanged the breech shut.

He pushed the ex-cook out of the way and dropped behind the firing lever. He had no time to use the telescopic sight. Making do as best he could, he flicked the adjustment to one hundred yards and pulled back the firing lever.

As the gun fired the trails rose abruptly and crashed down on the cobbles. A wave of hot air blasted in the top kick's face and the empty shell case rattled to the ground. But he had missed the target.

He heard the clang of metal as the ex-cook thrust home another shell. Swiftly he swung the gun back on target. Peering through the open sight, his hand sought the firing lever. But he never pulled it. Tracer pattered against the metal shield in front of him. A slug struck the nearside tyre. It exploded and the gun lurched to one side. 'Jesus!' the top kick cursed and took his hand away. The ex-cook staggered back screaming, his hand clutched to his bleeding face. Behind the top kick another soldier crumpled to the ground, his kneecap shattered.

Suddenly, amid a clatter of tank tracks, a Sherman came to a halt in the burning village square, clearly illuminated against the flames. The driver swung out of his hatch. For a moment the top kick crouching down with his wounded crew thought he was going to bug off. But the man took in the situation at once. He sprang into the turret and started to work the controls.

The commander of the big German Ferdinand SP buried in the rubble saw his danger at once. He ordered the motors started up and the SP began to draw back out of the ruin so that it could turn and face the Sherman with its fixed 88-mm.

But the Sherman gunner was quicker. A thin white flash sped towards the SP. The top kick saw the red glow as the 75-mm shell hit the German's side. The impact was tremendous. The Ferdinand rocked as if in a violent storm. An instant later it disappeared in a great sheet of red flame. No one got out.

The top kick got up and ran across to the Sherman. The man in the turret pulled himself from behind the gun and looked at the burning Ferdinand. 'I guess I arrived just in time,' he said.

'You betcha, feller,' the top kick shouted enthusiastically, 'regular old Seventh Cavalry stuff.' He stopped short. 'Hey, but where's your crew, Sarge?'

In reply he got another question, 'Is this the start-line for CCB?' the lone tanker asked.

'It was,' the top kick replied grimly and waved a dirty hand at the scene of death and destruction all around him. 'But Jesus, I don't know what General Dager's gonna say when he sees this mess.'

The other man nodded. 'Yeah, I know what you mean.' Then he explained. 'I had to pick this baby up from the replacement depot in Lux City. My crew is coming up with the rest of the battalion. We've been assigned to you guys to give you a bit of beef when you kick off. Where can I get her off the road? When the big wheels come, I don't want to get in their way.'

'Take it over there beyond the barn,' the top kick said. 'You'll be okay there. And say when we get that mess over there cleaned up come on over to the CP and grab yourself a cup of java.' He beamed up at the sergeant. 'And thanks again, feller.'

As the Sherman clattered off towards the barn, the top kick caught a glimpse of its Fourth divisional triangle and its name. He shook his head in mock disbelief. 'Christ those tank jockeys sure as hell give their tanks funny names – *Gruesome Twosome!* What next?'

II

Patton ordered Mims to stop. It still wasn't light yet, but the hissing Coleman lantern held by the medic told him that he had bumped into yet another incident on the road from Luxembourg City to the front. In spite of his age and the heavy protective clothing he was wearing in the open jeep, he swung himself out with surprising agility.

The medics had already begun to line the dead up along the side of the road. Others were working on the wounded. Patton bent close to a grey-haired corporal with a red armband who was pencilling the morphine dosage already given on a wounded man's forehead with an indelible crayon. He did so as if it gave him great personal pleasure; as it if it were worth doing well. 'What happened?'

The corporal did not look up. 'Krauts snuck up on 'em,' he said in a flat mid-western accent. 'Bush-whacked 'em as they was coming up the road. By the time we arrived, the Krauts had gone.'

Patton sighed. Another goddam incident! Ever since he and Mims had got over the frontier in Belgium, the night had been disturbed by sporadic firing. The Huns were putting in a lot of tip-and-run raids to try to disturb his build-up. He turned to Mims, 'Come on over here and give a hand. There's infantry coming up.'

The corporal turned and saw three big silver stars gleaming on the lacquered helmet. 'Jesus,' he breathed, his mouth dropping open. 'Old Blood and Guts!'

Patton ignored the comment. 'Help get the dead off the road, Corporal,' he said, 'there's infantry coming up. Don't want 'em to see this.'

Together the general and the two NCOs started to pull the remaining dead off the road. As the corporal passed on to the next immobile form and began pencilling in the morphine dose, Patton nodded to Mims.

They walked back to the jeep. 'It don't look too good, General,' Mims said, as he settled behind the wheel.

'It never does,' Patton replied.

As Mims pulled away and he was jerked back in his hard seat, George Patton knew that he must get to the front as soon as possible. The old Fourth was dead. If the new formation which masqueraded under its name was going to break through to Bastogne on time, as he had promised General Ike, it would need every bit of his energy and skill. 'Mims,' he snapped, his voice suddenly full of resolution, 'step on the gas. We've got a date – and I'm in a goddam hurry!'

III

Savage's team threw up the roadblock at the scene of the ambush five minutes after General Patton's jeep had vanished into the night, heading north to the sound of the guns.

He jumped out of the jeep while it was still moving, shouting to Smith, his arm strapped to his side, 'This'll be a good place!'

Behind them the half track, filled with what Smith could round up of the 12th's HQ Provost Company, ground to a halt. The MPs dropped over the side and waited for orders.

Savage took in the scene at a glance. The line of ambulances, with the sign CARRYING CASUALTIES faintly illuminated in their windows, their drivers smoking in the cabs; the heavy bridging equipment driven off the road waiting to be called for up front; the hastily erected pile of ammunition boxes; and the dead. It was the big push of 1918 all over again, he told himself. All that effort then, and at such cost – for what?

He turned to Smith who was out of the jeep waiting for orders. Savage waved his flashlight towards the crossroads. 'Get half of them up there,' he ordered. 'Spread them along the road – say, a hundred yards. When a convoy comes up, each soldier takes one truck. Make it thorough but snappy. I don't want old Blood and Guts breathing down my neck for holding up his beloved Fourth.'

Smith, obviously suffering from the loss of blood due to his wound, attempted a feeble grin. 'Yeah, we can't have that, Colonel.'

'I'll keep the rest up here as a reserve and spread a few of them out among the fields, just in case. And don't forget,' he added, as Smith turned to carry out his orders, 'keep a special watchout for a Sherman with "two" in its name. That old dame in Luxembourg swore that it had "two" something or other painted on it. Pity the old biddy couldn't read English.'

Swiftly they set about building their checkpoint, watched by curious medics, their task completed until the first casualties started streaming back from the front once the attack got underway in two hours' time.

Savage had just completed positioning his MPs in the fields on both sides of the road, checking the verges himself, his nerves jingling as he did so in case they were mined, when the first convoy came to a halt at the checkpoint.

He went over to the first driver himself. 'Who are you and where are you bound?' he asked, flashing his torch in the driver's face.

'Supply column for CCB, Fourth Armored,' the Service of Supply captain sitting next to the driver said. 'Say, what is this?' he added suspiciously. Then he caught a glimpse of Savage's silver eagles. 'Sorry sir. I didn't recognise your rank. Is anything the matter?'

Savage ignored the query. 'Did you come through Luxembourg City?'

'Yes sir.'

'Stop?'

'Not even for a cup of java, Colonel,' the driver commented bitterly, beating the officer to it, 'and I've been at this darn wheel since six o'clock yesterday morning.'

'Did you stop on the way?' Savage ignored the driver and coldly repeated his question.

'No sir,' the captain said. He turned to the driver and said severely, 'Watch your manners, Olson. You might get a sudden up-grading to rifleman – as of tomorrow.'

'In a pig's eye!' the driver snarled.

'Knock it off,' Savage ordered. He raised his voice so that the MPs, lining the road with their carbines and tommy guns at the ready, heard. 'All right, check out each driver – and have a look in the backs!'

The captain looked alarmed. 'It's as much as my job's worth if I'm late up front, Colonel,' he pleaded.

Olson laughed. 'You might get a sudden promotion, like to CO of a rifle company!'

Savage did not wait to hear the captain's reply. He started to supervise the checking of the long line of ammunition trucks.

Gerling knew that something was wrong when the trucks stopped and he heard the stamp of heavy feet on the frozen snow outside. The sound could only be that of a cop; the sound was the same the whole world over.

He rose stiffly from his cramped position between the boxes of 75-mm tank ammunition and peered out of the canvas that covered the end of the truck.

White-helmeted MPs were working their way down the line, flickering their flashlights up and down the trucks' mud-scattered outlines, stopping to check the drivers and the insides of the vehicles. The nearest 'snowdrop', armed with a tommy gun was only twenty yards away. He could see him outlined distinctly in the flashlight of the MP behind him, as he examined the vehicle next to the one he had hidden in ever since he had taken his life in his hands and jumped on to it as it passed under a low railway bridge on the outskirts of the capital.

Gerling's heart sank. It looked like this was the end of the road. But then a vision of Hartmann's mad twisted face flashed before his mind's eye. Was he going to get away with it after all? No, the bastard was not. He must find some way out. He felt the Colt at his hip. He could drop the MP easily. But what then?

There were too many of them – and there'd been too many deaths already. He had to do it some other way. An idea flashed through his mind and he pulled out the big pistol, praying that the windscreen glass of *Ami* trucks was no better than that of the *Wehrmacht*. Carefully pulling aside the canvas, he aimed and fired in the same instant.

The glass of the truck beyond the one where the MP was standing questioning the driver splintered, disappearing in a sudden cobweb. The MP dropped the flashlight. Someone cursed. A whistle blew and a voice yelled 'Over here!'

Gerling dropped over the tail on to the snow. He crashed through a hedge and started running through the snowed-up field.

'He's there!' a voice shouted behind him.

A dozen flashlights turned on him. A shot rang out. Then a voice commanded 'Don't fire! It might not be him!'

Gerling stumbled on. Behind him Colonel Savage cupped his hands and shouted, 'Whoever you are, don't go any further. There's a minefield out there. Do you hear – MINES!'

A flashlight flicked on and ran ahead of him, its light slicing the darkness between the dark firs fifty metres ahead of him. To his horror Gerling saw the voice was right. He could see the familiar white tapes which indicated the extent of the mine-clearing squads and beyond them the board with the skull and crossbones. He did not need to read the warning. He knew well what it would be: ATTENTION – ACHTUNG – DANGER. Whatever the language, the words meant sudden and terrible mutilation.

Behind him Savage shouted, 'All right then, come on back with your hands up – and slow!'

He started to turn but again Hartmann's crazy face loomed up in front of him and he knew he must go on.

'All right, drop the bastard!' a voice yelled.

A tommy gun made a pattern in the snow at his heels. Twisting and turning, Gerling headed for the woods of death ahead. A carbine joined in the fire. His chest heaving uncontrollably, his mouth wide open as he gasped for air, Gerling flung himself into the dark trees, heedless of the mines, sprawling full length under the cover of their snow-laden branches. The lights suddenly went out.

IV

General Patton shouted to Mims to stop as the first stragglers appeared in the thin white light which came from the slits of their headlights. The jeep squealed to a stop only feet away from the first group of men.

Before Patton could ask what the men were doing, a German 88 opened up from close by. A straggler fell into the snow howling, his leg suddenly gone. A bareheaded sergeant standing next to him started to scream. He broke away from the rest and threw himself into the ditch. Patton shouted to Mims to help the wounded soldier.

He strode over to the infantry sergeant. 'What's up, son?' he asked solicitously.

The man's eyes did not even register his presence. He continued to scream, the saliva dripping down his unshaven chin.

'Soldier,' he said in his harshest voice, 'snap to!'

No effect.

Firmly he strode back to the jeep and pulled out Mims' carbine from the bucket holster. He slapped it into the hands of the first soldier he saw. 'You,' he snapped, 'what's your name?'

'De Maggio, sir,' the man stuttered.

'All right, de Maggio, you're now Corporal – Corporal de Maggio, I want you to get these men organised, do you hear?'

The fat PFC with a dirty bandage round his head answered uncertainly with a hesitant 'Yes sir.'

'All right, get a couple of your men to stay here with that poor fellow.' He pointed to the dying soldier on the road. 'The rest of you get back the way you came. We need every man in the line; you know that, Corporal, don't you?'

'Yes sir.' This time the answer came with alacrity.

'There'll be a collecting point for fellows like you where you'll get fresh weapons,' Patton said. 'As for that yeller-belly,' he pointed to the sergeant cringing in the ditch, 'I want you to hand him over to the first MP you meet. If he tries to escape, shoot him. You have my approval. A coward like that could have a terrible effect on young soldiers.'

The new corporal nodded his agreement.

Patton strode back to the jeep. 'All right, Mims, let's go.'

Behind them the corporal started to issue his orders. As the jeep drew away, Mims could hear him bullying the bareheaded sergeant out of the ditch.

Patton breathed out hard. 'You know, Mims,' he said after a few minutes. 'It's appalling to see a man break like that in battle. It's worse than watching a death watching the breakdown of a man's spirit and pride – all that gives meaning and purpose to life.'

'Yes, General,' Mims answered dutifully, only half understanding the Old Man's words. But when he dared risk a glance at the Third Army Commander, he noted in the faint red glow from the dash that the General's hands were shaking.

V

Gerling crawled forward. His hands and knees were frozen for the temperature was well below zero. He longed to stop and blow on his hands, to warm his aching fingers, but he knew he could not stop. Time was running out and he was miles from the real front.

He raised the twig he had snapped off a pine and prodded it in the snow. Nothing happened. He crawled on another pace. Another five minutes passed and he was beginning to hope that he had come to the end of the minefield. The noise of the traffic on the road had died away to a steady distant buzz. Surely whoever had laid it would not have extended it so far from the road.

He stopped with a jerk. For a moment he thought he had stumbled into a German position. In the moonlight he could make out at least a dozen men sitting, crouching or lying full length, their weapons slung over their shoulders, as if they were just about to set out on a patrol. Then he saw the missing limbs, the severed foot lying on the surface of the blood-stained snow. They were all dead, frozen already into a rigid, waxen-faced tableau of horror!

Very carefully he began to crawl towards them. He reached a green-smocked soldier, caught in the moment of death, his body frozen upright. Gingerly he circled another dead man in the green camouflaged smock of the SS, his body sprawled full length. Then he stopped abruptly. A row of tiny prongs ran out to the left of the dead SS man. In the silver light he could see them quite clearly. Carefully he backed away and crawled to the right of the body. Again the prongs. Anti-personnel mines. 'De-bollockers,' the *Amis* called them. He knew that from his day with the *Ami* prisoners at Moosberg; they were the most feared of German weapons.

The slightest pressure and the little mine exploded, hurling out a score or more of steel balls at the height of the human groin. The result was catastrophic. 'Ya should have seen the guy next to me when it hit him,' a round-eyed GI prisoner had whispered in awe when he had related the story to Gerling, 'they dragged him out later. But he had no nuts left!'

Cautiously Gerling reached out over the dead SS man towards the next body. His palms smoothed the surface of the snow, swinging with painful slowness from left to right, his heart thumping as he waited for the contact with the metal plunger and the explosion which would follow. But nothing happened.

Gingerly he pulled himself over the body of the dead SS man. It felt like a log of wood. He had just cleared it when a sudden soft sound paralysed him with terror. At the back of his head the hairs stood out on the nape of his neck. Then a brown head, with a white blaze down the brow, peered out at him through the branches. Again the cow mooed.

Stiffly Gerling rose to his feet. With a frozen hand he wiped the beads of sweat from his brow and heaved a long sigh of relief. He knew now he was safe. The drill was routine. They had perfected it in Russia with the pigs and goats they had found running loose in the villages. He pulled out his pistol and stuck it in the opening of his blouse. He undid his belt and approached the cow, muttering what he hoped were soothing noises. The animal did not move, even when he fastened the belt around its tail. Obviously it had wandered from some abandoned farmhouse, perhaps stampeded into the snowy fields by the barrage. As Gerling urged it to turn round with encouraging noises and the weight of his shoulder against its skinny flanks, he thanked God that it was not a bull.

Finally he got it round, facing the snowy fields ahead. He pulled off a fir switch. 'Come on,' he said and flicked it across the rump. Slowly it moved forward. Gerling waited till its tail was stretched out as far as it would go, held up by his belt. Thus he had a distance of just over a metre between himself and the animal's rump. If the poor beast did stand on a mine, its belly would take the full blast, while he would be relatively safe from the deadly steel balls.

'Giddy up,' he urged. The cow lumbered on. Slowly the strange procession set out across the silent fields.

VI

More and more trucks and jeeps pulling little trailers loaded with cannon shells bumped over the frozen road and swung off to left and right at the command of the red-faced, frozen MPs. The first of the tanks clanked up and were directed to the fields on the left of the barn.

'Them your guys?' the bareheaded top kick asked. Hartmann, canteen cup in hand, shook his head. 'No, that must be some other outfit.' His eyes took in the scene – the ambulances with the wounded on stretchers on top, the graves registration men trying to hack holes in the iron-hard earth to bury the dead, a bunch of Negro soldiers busy unloading ammunition in the field. 'They should be here soon. When does the brass arrive anyway?'

The top kick held up his watch to catch the light of the moon. 'It's five-thirty. They should be here any minute.'

A jeep was bumping its way slowly over the rutted road. Over in the ditch, the NCOs and squad commanders were chivvying the survivors of the armoured infantry company into some sort of order. Time and again a young soldier would fall out and urinate. The top kick shook his head in disbelief. 'Willya look at them guys, Sarge,' he said in mock sadness, 'they'll cream their pants before they even see a Kraut!'

Hartmann gave a taut smile.

'Well, feller, look after yourself. I guess I'd better get over and see what I can do with them heroes.' He nodded to Hartmann, picked up his carbine and strolled over to where his men were forming up for the attack. But Hartmann had no eyes for him. His gaze was fixed on the jeep. It stopped and an officer with an injured arm stepped out. A moment later he was joined from the other side of the jeep by a portly officer in a dirty white trenchcoat.

Hartmann knew that the general also wore a white trenchcoat, but this wasn't him; he was too small. Yet Hartmann did not dismiss them altogether. Obviously they did not belong to the combat troops for they made no attempt to join the soldiers in the ditch.

A larger bridging unit jolted by. For a

moment he lost the two officers from view and when the huge trailer had finally passed, they had separated. The older one was walking over to the squad of Shermans lined up in the field. The other was coming in his direction.

Hartmann decided it was time to go. The cooks were still serving hot C-ration hash and coffee. Perhaps the officer with the injured arm was heading for food and drink. If he were, Hartmann did not want to get involved in conversation with him. He had no time for idle chatter. His mind was full of the task ahead.

He turned and strode off to where he had parked the *Gruesome Twosome,* in the little cobbled side street, fifty yards from the smoking Ferdinand, the armour of which still glowed a dull red. It was an ideal site. With his cannon he could cover the cross-roads where the barn was located off the main road from the south. Even if he missed with his first shot there was no room in the narrow side street for an enemy tank to man-oeuvre against him. Even infantry armed with bazookas would have a job to get close to him. The houses on both sides were shat-tered wrecks, offering little cover for infil-trating infantry. Hartmann's lips twisted in a sneer. 'Those *Amis,*' he told himself, 'haven't the courage of a chicken. They wouldn't dare attempt to tackle me without artillery support.' He stopped by the Sherman and surveyed his position. It was virtually impregnable. He could sweep the length of the little back road and the crossing beyond with impunity. He was in complete mastery of the situation. Satisfied, he clambered up on the turret of the *Gruesome Twosome* and began to make his last preparations for the killing.

'Sergeant,' the voice was hesitant, too educated to achieve the decisive tone needed for a command.

Hartmann spun round. The officer with the injured arm was standing below, staring up at him curiously.

Hartmann took a pace backwards so that his face fell into the shadow cast by the ruined wall behind him. Down below the icy light glinted on the sphinx on the young officer's collar.

Hartmann recognised the insignia of the enemy's counter-intelligence service.

'Yes sir,' he said, as steadily as he could. 'Can I help you?'

'Are you in charge of that tank, Sergeant?'

Hartmann could see the officer's hand resting on the butt of his stub-nosed thirty-eight. His own grease gun was in the turret. Attempting to be casual, he pulled off the clips attaching the spade to the side of the turret. 'No, sir, I was just going to borrow this.' He indicated the spade.

The officer looked up at him warily, as he freed the second clip.

'What do you want it for?' he asked.

'Hell, sir, I can see you haven't been long at the front.'

'What do you mean?' the officer said testily.

'Well, sir,' Hartmann said conversationally, turning around and towering over the officer looking up at him. 'When you grab a spade in the line, you're off somewhere by yourself. Do you get me?' He held up the spade, as if to show the officer.

'Not quite, Sergeant.'

'Well, sir, to go for a crap. Hygiene you know.'

The officer's mouth opened and he started to express his understanding when Hartmann brought the spade down blade foremost.

The blade bit deep into his skull and he went down without a sound.

Hartmann dropped from the tank. He glanced swiftly up and down the little side street but there was no one in sight. He grabbed the dead man by the shoulders and dragged him into the shadows. With the back of his foot, he kicked open the door of one of the shattered cottages and pushed the corpse into the darkness.

As he hurried back to the tank, he heard the faint but distinct sound of motors getting ever closer. He glanced at his watch. It was nearly six. It must be him!

Savage hurried over to the jeep.

'General Dager,' he said.

Dager, commander of the CCB, turned and peered at him. 'Yes, what do you want?'

Savage introduced himself and silently wished that Smith had not suddenly got himself lost. He understood the mentality of these Third Army guys better than Savage did.

'So you see, sir, we of the OSS believe that an attempt is going to be made on the life of General Patton,' he concluded his brief resumé.

Dager looked at him as if he were some rookie who had gone on parade at Fort Benning without his pants and he were the inspecting officer.

'Do you seriously mean to tell me that one of your agents was working with the Krauts and now they're roaming somewhere behind our lines with a tank to kill General Patton? What the hell do you canteen commandos think goes on at the front?'

Behind him his staff officers turned and looked at them curiously. Savage felt himself going red.

'I'm trying to run a goddam war, Colonel, not ... not,' he stuttered for the right words, 'play a role in some lousy spy movie! Go and see my intelligence man. I haven't got time for you now. General Patton is due in a few minutes.'

Dager turned and walked back to his officers. Together the little group, followed at a respectful distance by the bodyguard, moved off and Savage was left standing alone.

VII

The fat coloured corporal hit the brakes and the truck skidded to a stop at the edge of the village, where a group of coloured artillerymen were unloading shell canisters for their 'long Toms'. He grinned proudly, showing a mouthful of gold teeth. 'There ya are, soldier. This is the end of the line.'

Gerling jerked himself out of his daze and his hand flashed to his pistol. Then, realising where he was, he let go of it again somewhat foolishly.

The corporal grinned. 'Kinda nervy, eh,' he said.

'Don't worry, the big war ain't started yet. It's up there.' He pointed to the traffic-lined road sneaking into the village. 'If you wants it. This baby's happy enough to stay here. That's close enough to the scene for me. I's no hero.'

'Thanks,' Gerling said and dropped out of

the cab. The artillerymen came forward at once and began pulling off the boxes of ammunition.

Gerling hurried down the village street. Everywhere were signs of the attack soon to come – trucks full of supplies, ambulances and recovery vehicles, jeeps buzzing back and forth laden with ammunition, signalmen stringing up radio communications and engineers repairing the white tape on both sides of the road to indicate that the verges had been cleared of mines.

A hundred yards ahead of him infantry started to get out of a group of open trucks. They stood around in their heavy equipment, their young faces bewildered and frightened like sheep being led to the slaughter. Gerling quickened his pace.

'All right,' the NCOs were shouting, 'get them packs off and form up! This is it, guys!'

Obediently they did as they were ordered; dropping their heavy equipment on the snow they formed up on either side of the road. Gerling joined them. No one seemed to notice.

A fat young lieutenant who looked all of eighteen walked down the column looking at their faces with unseeing eyes. At the head of the column, he hitched up his pistol-belt and waved his hand. 'Okay, men, let's go!' he shouted.

The column moved forward.

Slowly and deliberately they plodded up the sides of the road, moving through the village. Before them the flicker of the permanent barrage grew an ever deeper pink. The noise of the guns intensified. They marched on, each man keeping his own uneven step. A yellow light flashed from the door of one of the wrecked cottages. A soldier in shirt sleeves looked out. His hand gripped a dripping ladle. A cook. He watched them straggle by without interest, as if they were not there.

A group of officers barred the way. Maps in hands, they stood in the frozen mud and snow, waving their arms importantly, clicking their tongues like teachers on a schoolyard because the children were moving into the classrooms too slowly. The column swung left. A colonel in a dirty white trenchcoat watched them, his eyes behind the gold-rimmed glasses sad and paternal.

Up front a heavy American machine gun started to chatter like some jackdaw, trying to bore into an impossibly hard tree trunk. A moment later came the high-pitched burr of a German spandau. A white rocket shot into the air, and hung there for a moment, bathing everything in its eerie light. They moved on like automatons, as if their whole previous existence had been merely preparation for this one moment.

'Hold it there,' the fat lieutenant bellowed

and held up his hand. 'Traffic coming up!'

The soldiers stepped into the ditch and a moment later an armoured car swept by, four MPs squatting on its metal deck, frozen and miserable, their mittened fingers on the triggers of their carbines. Behind a jeep bounced up and down on the shell-pocked road. Gerling caught a glimpse of a thin face above an immaculate white trenchcoat, and a lacquered helmet which shone in the light of the fat lieutenant's torch as he waved the jeep on. The helmet bore three silver stars.

They plodded on. The small arms fire grew in volume. Flares began to shoot up along the German line. They filed past a little crowd of officers who had collected around the convoy which had overtaken them a few moments ago.

Then the first German shell hit the village. The fat lieutenant dropped to one knee in surprise. The man behind him blundered into him. 'God darn and dammit,' someone shouted in the confusion, as the whole column came to an awkward stop. 'Can't the hell you watch where you're going?' Flames started to lick upwards from the house which had been hit. They were tinged with a fierce yellow light. The house had probably been used to store gasoline, Gerling thought.

At the same moment he turned his head and saw the tank. The sudden glare lit it up as it crouched in the shadows. He knew it at once. It was the *Gruesome Twosome!* Slowly its cannon began to swing in the direction of the little group of officers standing round the jeep.

The column had sorted itself out and started to move forward again. Gerling did not hesitate. 'Got to take a piss,' he said to the man behind him and dropped out. The man muttered something and plodded on blindly. Gerling ran down the cobbled street towards the *Gruesome Twosome.*

Patton raised his voice above the chatter of the machine guns, 'Well, Dager,' he said staring straight ahead as if he could see something there known only to himself. 'I guess it's in your hands now. I want you to go like hell for Bastogne! Do you understand?'

'Yes sir!'

Behind them the Shermans which were to cover the first wave of infantry burst into life. The group of senior officers standing at the crossroads saw the flames shoot from their exhausts as tank after tank started. Behind them the 'long Toms' opened up with a deafening crash. The first salvo of 105-mm shells soared over their heads. The terrible symphony of war had begun.

'Hartmann!' Gerling screamed above the roar, but there was no reply from within the turret. It was as if the tank were abandoned.

But Gerling knew that the SS major was crouched behind the gunsight ready to fire at any moment. Drawing his pistol he hammered with his butt on the turret. The cover swung back and Hartmann stood there, staring at Gerling's face in blank incomprehension.

'Gerling! I thought they had you,' he said slowly. His body was rigidly tense – like that of a soldier Gerling had seen on the Russian front, who had run amok after sixty days of continuous combat. His comrades had been forced to shoot him in the end.

'Hartmann, stop this. It's all over. We've lost.' Gerling raised his voice against the roar of the guns. *'We've lost, Hartmann!'*

'Lost?' he cried. 'You say *that!* You...' His rage overcame him and he couldn't speak for a second. 'You're like the rest – weak! But I shall never give up–'

Gerling aimed and fired. The slug ricocheted off the turret, a foot below Hartmann's outstretched hand. Gerling's second shot missed him by inches. Next moment the cover fell with a hollow clang. Hartmann had closed himself in.

Gerling heard the faint hum as the electric turret mechanism started to operate and the long gun slowly began to move. He glanced up the road. The generals were shaking hands. They would be gone in a minute. But for the moment, they were completely in

Hartmann's power.

Gerling glanced round and saw the wrecked anti-tank gun, slumped to one side where a shell had caught the wheel. It was his only hope. He pelted towards it and flung himself behind the breech. The breech pin was thrust out. The little gun was loaded. With a thrust of his right shoulder, he swung the long barrel round until it was pointing towards the Sherman. He groped under it till he found the firing lever. Squinting through the open sight, he jerked it back hard. The gun erupted under his armpit. The trails rose and crashed to the cobbles again. A wave of hot air hit him in the face like a flabby fist. He coughed, and blinked his eyes. As the empty shell case rattled to the ground, he saw to his horror that he'd missed.

Hartmann reacted at once to the new danger. The turret swung round smoothly. A 75-mm armour-piercing shell tore through the air and struck a house only twenty feet away from Gerling. Feverishly Gerling scrambled to the other side of the gun, tore out the remaining shell clamped to the metal shield, and thrust it into the gaping breech, noticing that blood had begun to drip from his sleeve.

Across the road, Hartmann had swung the turret round to bear once more on the group now dispersing at the crossroads. This was his last chance.

'Mine too!' Gerling said to himself.

Desperately he swung the gun round until the sights showed the rear end near the Sherman's vulnerable gasoline engine. Carefully this time, trying to control his nerves, he squeezed the firing lever. The gun roared back. Huge metal shards flew through the air as the *Gruesome Twosome* rocked like a ship in a hurricane. Gerling closed his eyes against the glare. A dull roar filled the little back street, as the vehicles at the crossroads moved away. Slowly as the general's jeep bounced by he slipped to the cobbles, wet with the blood from his injured arm.

A battle does not stop when the shooting stops. The men and women who survive go on to live and die at their own appointed places and times.

Gerling survived. A 4th Armored dentist, who happened to be visiting the front 'for kicks' stopped the bleeding and saved Gerling's life. The dentist was shot and killed almost immediately afterwards by a stray 5th Para sniper as he came out of the barn, somewhat shaken and dazed by his first – and last – frontline operation.

For a while he was kept in the special camp established in France for the newly captured POWs of the *Liebstandarte*, suspected of having taken part in the so-called 'Malmédy Massacre'. In 1946 he was transferred to

Dachau Camp for trial, where somehow or other he convinced the prosecutor of the 'SS Criminals', Colonel Rosenfeld, that he was a genuine case. His sentence, as a result, was only four years.

In 1948 he escaped with the aid of the ODESSA organisation and taking the 'B-B' route (Bremen-Bari) fled to Brazil, where over the years he started a new life rising to become a senior manager in *Volkswagen Brasil*. About three years ago he set up his own export-import agency and, after his first visit to the Federal Republic when he spent a week listening to the debates on the new 'East Agreements' between West Germany and the German Democratic Republic, returned to South America to take an active part in right-wing politics. Today he is an important figure in a group of ageing ex-SS men and German political refugees who still cling to the belief that time can be turned back.

His one-time chief, Otto Skorzeny, surrendered to the Allies in 1945. An immediate investigation was launched – at Eisenhower's express order – into his role in the attempted assassination. Under severe pressure from Colonel Rosenfeld and his own lawyer, Lt Colonel Robert Durst, appointed to defend him by the US Army, Skorzeny steadfastly denied that there had been any plot to assassinate Eisenhower. As he assured Rosenfeld, if he *had* been given such an order, he would have done his utmost to carry out the task. But he hadn't! As far as the other Allied generals were concerned, he knew nothing of plots to kill them.

Thus Allied Counter-Intelligence heads concluded that the plot to kill Patton had been worked out and passed on to Hartmann by Baron von Foelkersam, Skorzeny's chief aide, who had far more experience of clandestine operations than his commander. But the CIC was unable to grill Foelkersam; he had disappeared in the last fighting on the Eastern Front.

In early 1948 Skorzeny himself disappeared from his internment camp, appearing some time later in Spain. He settled down – apparently – to the routine life of a businessman in the Spanish capital, though he was suspected of taking part in a plot to kill Stalin with a poison bullet in the mid-fifties. There was also some talk of arms smuggling to Egypt. But by the sixties Skorzeny was a respectably established businessman again. In early 1970 he was stricken by two tumours of the spine. But he survived the operation and, after some months of paralysis, managed to learn to walk again. Today he lives in Madrid, visited from time to time by admiring former members of his organisation, who come from all over Western Europe – and occasionally from Eastern Europe as well.

Colonel Savage returned to his desk job in Wall Street after helping Allen Dulles to set up the CIA, the successor of the OSS. He didn't like it. In 1965 her was divorced, after some unpleasant publicity about his affair with a young actress from an off-Broadway show. He took to wearing his hair long and gave up his gold-rimmed glasses for contact lenses. In 1967 he was stabbed to death in the cold-water flat lived in by his current girl-friend, a student, when trying to stop a 16-year-old coloured drug addict from rifling her purse. It contained exactly two dollars fifty.

No one came to his funeral.

And the General? Three months after his Third Army had helped to smash the remaining might of National Socialist Germany, General Eisenhower relieved him of his command because of the way he ran Bavaria, his part of Occupied Germany. He was given the Fifteenth US Army, which existed in name only. For several weeks, he moped about and read a great deal, taking trips all over Europe to accept yet another medal or award from the local worthies of some town that the Third Army had liberated in the heady days of the previous year. As November gave way to December, General Patton became increasingly restless and tense. It was obvious that he was going through a period of gnawing and deep turmoil.

In the first week of December, 1945, he told his one-eyed Chief-of-Staff 'Hap' Gay, who had been with him throughout the campaign, that he was going to resign from the Army and that he was 'going to do it with a statement that will be remembered a long time. I am determined to be free to live my own way of life and I'm going to make that unforgettably clear.'

To take his mind off the subject, Gay suggested a hunting trip. The two generals took off on the morning of 9 December, 1945. It was a raw, cold and overcast day – not much different from the kind of weather the two of them had encountered the year before in the Ardennes. Patton's soldier-driver, 20-year-old Horace Woodring, who had replaced Mims four months before (today he's a prosperous used car dealer in Detroit) drove carefully. But even though he was only doing 30 mph and he and Gay were not scratched when he crashed into the back of an Army truck just outside Mannheim, General Patton was seriously injured.

'What a hell of a way to die,' he heard Patton whisper to Gay. 'I think I'm paralysed. I can't move my arm. Rub it, will you?'

A wave of rumours that Patton had been 'fixed' ran through the US Army in Occupied Germany. Hearing of the 'accident' in far-off Massachusetts, Fred Ayer's first reaction was, 'Accident hell. It was murder.

Those Communist son-of-bitches killed him!' Fred Ayers was Patton's nephew and had been his special agent in Europe during the war.

But if an inquiry was ever launched into the 'accident', nothing is known of it. The driver of the truck tried to commit suicide, but was prevented just in time. In the end, Ayer decided that 'it was not murder; it was fate'.

For twelve days General Patton fought for his life in the *Lazarett* in Heidelberg, where Gerling had been recruited for the plan to assassinate him. (One of the men who fetched and carried for the British specialist who tried to save the General's life was the doctor who had passed on the leaflet to Gerling; but by now he had been reduced to the rank of orderly.) On the afternoon of 21 December, he whispered to his wife, 'It's too dark. I mean too late.' Two hours later he was dead.

A special train took his body to Luxembourg for burial in the US military cemetery at Hamm, just outside the little capital. In pouring rain he was laid to rest among the graves of 6,000 soldiers who had been killed in action with his Third Army. It was Christmas Eve, 1945 – one year to the day after his Fourth Armored Division had broken the back of the German offensive in the Ardennes by relieving Bastogne.

The publishers hope that this book has given you enjoyable reading. Large Print Books are especially designed to be as easy to see and hold as possible. If you wish a complete list of our books please ask at your local library or write directly to:

Dales Large Print Books
Magna House, Long Preston,
Skipton, North Yorkshire.
BD23 4ND

This Large Print Book, for people
who cannot read normal print,
is published under the auspices of

THE ULVERSCROFT FOUNDATION

... we hope you have enjoyed this book.
Please think for a moment about those
who have worse eyesight than you ...
and are unable to even read or enjoy
Large Print without great difficulty.

You can help them by sending a
donation, large or small, to:

**The Ulverscroft Foundation,
1, The Green, Bradgate Road,
Anstey, Leicestershire, LE7 7FU,
England.**
or request a copy of our brochure for
more details.

The Foundation will use all donations
to assist those people who are visually
impaired and need special attention
with medical research, diagnosis
and treatment.

Thank you very much for your help.